John Fitzgerald Murphy

A Bit O' Blarney

An Irish Play of the Present Time, in Three Acts

John Fitzgerald Murphy

A Bit O' Blarney
An Irish Play of the Present Time, in Three Acts

ISBN/EAN: 9783744740456

Printed in Europe, USA, Canada, Australia, Japan

Cover: Foto ©Andreas Hilbeck / pixelio.de

More available books at **www.hansebooks.com**

A BIT O' BLARNEY

WALTER H. BAKER & CO.
BOSTON

Something New, Funny and Refined.

PROF. BAXTER'S

GREAT INVENTION,

— OR —

OLD MAIDS MADE NEW.

A COMEDY-FARCE IN ONE ACT.

By MARY B. HORNE,

Author of "THE PEAK SISTERS," "THE CARNIVAL OF DAYS," "THE BOOK OF DRILLS, Parts I and II," ETC.

For three male and three female characters. Modern every-day costumes. Scenery of the very simplest character. Plays about an hour, or longer, according to specialties, songs, etc., introduced This entertainment is a decided novelty and is excruciatingly funny. First-rate Irish soubrette part, and capital comic old man. Prof. Baxter's patent process for making old people young again suits everybody, both on the stage and off.

Price, - - - - 15 cents.

SYNOPSIS.

SCENE.— Dr. Baxter's Office. Mary Ann and the Professor. A scientific breakfast. Patients. A sweet young thing of fifty. Mary Ann romances. The old dude. More patients. A back number. Getting ready for the operation. Roxanna and the Doctor. Greek meets Greek. Electro-motive force *vs.* a female tongue. The "gossimeres." The current begins to work. Woolley has a very strange feeling. Charged with electricity. "I never charge, but take cash down." Filling the cabinets. A little backward in coming forward. Dorothy's shyness. "What, get in there with two men!" Mary Ann sacrificed to propriety. Roxanna and the Doctor again. Getting the mitten. "You press the button, and I'll do the rest." The current full on. Groans of the wounded. After the battle. Old maids and old dudes made new. Roxanna's work undone. "It's a deep laid plot!" Celebrating the event. "The dude who couldn't dance." Mary Ann and "The Irish Jubilee." It is in the air and Roxanna catches it. A terrible catastrophe. The deaf old gentlemen gets overdone. The Professor adopts the old infant. Marrying and giving in marriage. The "invention" pronounced a grand success.

Walter H. Baker & Co., 23 Winter St., Boston.

A BIT O' BLARNEY

AN IRISH PLAY OF THE PRESENT TIME

In Three Acts

BY

FITZGERALD MURPHY

AUTHOR OF "SHAMROCK AND ROSE," "THE IRISH STATESMAN," ETC.

———

BOSTON

Walter H. Baker & Co

160234

1893

CHARACTERS.

(AS ORIGINALLY PERFORMED AT THE PARK THEATRE, LOS ANGELES, CAL.,
APRIL 10, 1893.)

RODY THE ROVER, *a bit of Irish sunshine* . . . . FITZGERALD MURPHY
CUDDEEN CASSIDY, *a creature of circumstances* . . FRANK M. READICK
SQUIRE ROSSMORE, *an usurper* . . . . . . FRANK C. THOMPSON
EDWARD LAWTON, *a California lawyer* . . . . A. C. SUTHERLAND
TEDDY BURKE, *his own servant* . . . . . . FRANK DE CAMP
CAPTAIN CASTLETON, *of the Royal Dragoons* . . . MAURICE SHARPLEIGH
CORKERRY, *a cockney sergeant* . . . . J. L. AMES
DARBEY DARNEY, *an antiquated relic of lost boyhood* . . GRANT FROMAN
ROSALEEN O'CONNOR, *a sweet flower from an Irish hillside,*
MISS GEORGIE WOODTHORPE
LADY PATRICE, *Rody's sister* . . . . . . MISS MILLIE FREEMAN
SHEVAUN JACK, *a widow with a shebeen* . . MISS ALMA SHYMER
Peasants, Soldiers, and Police.

COPYRIGHT, 1893, BY WALTER H. BAKER & CO.

All Rights Reserved.

THE ORIGINAL MUSIC

Of this play is not published or for sale. Any airs may be substituted to suit the tastes of the performers.

2

COSTUMES.

Rody the Rover. Gray ragged coat, breeches, and leggings, gray shooting-cap, red flannel shirt, and loose necktie. In last act he dresses in neat corduroy breeches and blue stockings, flowered waistcoat, and dons Squire's smoking-robe.

Mr. Lawton. White sombrero hat and modern gray business suit.

Teddy Burke. Irish peasant dress, knee-breeches, etc.

Squire Rossmore. Modern stylish English dress, silk hat, Prince Albert coat, etc.

Cuddeen Cassidy. Irish peasant dress, battered hat, old-fashioned swallow tails, breeches and leggings, and dark flannel shirt.

Capt. Castleton. Either English officer's costume of red and gold, or black costume of Royal Irish Constabulary.

Corkerry. A sergeant's regimentals (comic make-up).

Darby Darney. Black knee-breeches, waistcoat, white shirt, and comic hat. Woollen stockings and low-cut shoes.

Rosaleen. Irish peasant girl's dress (long to ankles), and cloak with hood thrown back. Colors selected.

Lady Patrice. Act I. Green riding-habit. Act II. Lady's white summer dress. Act III. Household *negligée.*

Shevaun. Comedy old woman make-up. Rough peasant dress.

PROPERTY LIST.

Act I. Furze tree with yellow blossoms fixed on; grass mats; lots of artificial flowers; two little whiskey kegs; horse-hoof effect; little black box containing sealed document; blackthorn stick for RODY; cigars for SQUIRE and LAWTON; little piece of black stone for "Bit o' Blarney"; snare-drum on stage; six guns; one loaded gun; cartridge; artificial rose and "shamrock" for RODY; sword.

Act II. Two tables; basin of water outside of window, and handkerchief; blackthorn for Castleton; chairs; one three-legged stool; old fiddle and bow; sand for dancing; mattress outside window; kettle to hang in fireplace; lampblack for sides of kettle, bottles for bar; glasses for drinking; clubs for peasants; little jar — a cruiskeen; wreath of white flowers and green for ROSALEEN; cupboard with cups, etc.; tin basin full of soaped water; candle in candlestick (on table); matches (on table).

Act III. Writing-desk and chair; papers, pen, and ink; document (sealed); two lamps (lighted); sofa; decanter of brandy; glass of brandy and soda; three pistols; knife for CASSIDY; black box with little stone; wallet with notes for SQUIRE.

LIGHT PLOT.

ACT I.

Lights one-quarter down.

Cue. —— "Guard it wid my life."
Lights three-fourths down slowly.

Cue. —— "Murdher! I'm kilt!"
Flash up lights for a second, thunder effect.

Cue. —— "It's a lie!"
Flash all lights up for Curtain.

ACT II.

Lights full up.

Cue. —— "My sweet Rosaleen." (*Exit* RODY, C.)
Lights one-half down. When Rosaleen lights candle, turn up lights till end of act.

ACT III.

Scene I. —Lights all up.

Scene II. —Lights one-half down.

Cue. —— "Damn him!"
Lights three-fourths down.

Cue. —— "I hope so."
Lights one-half up when Patrice enters with lamp.

Cue. —— "Heaven defend us!!!"
Lights three-fourths down quick (very important).

Cue. —— "Return in the morning."
Lights up one-half when Lawton turns up lamp.

Cue. —— "My eccentric friend."
Lights all up till end of act.

SYNOPSIS.

Act I. Glen Blarney by moonlight. Old-fashioned love-making. The arrival of the American. The rescue. The first chapter in an international romance. A story of California. Rody and the leprehaun. The story of Rosaleen. The black bird and the dove. The blow. Love under the furze-blossoms. The trust. The robbery and the murder. THE ACCUSATION.

Act II. Shevaun's shebeen at sunset. The May-Day festivities. The Queen o' the May. Cuddeen Cassidy falls into the wrong company. The old, old story. Lord and peasant. The proposal. The story of the murder. Arrival of the police. The parting. THE ARREST.

Act III. Blarney Manor. "The darkest hour is that before the dawn." A California game of bluff. The murderer and the ghost. The widow's predicament. The conspirators. THE BIT O' BLARNEY. Rosaleen's peril. The attempted assassination. The tables turned. SQUIRE RODY.

4

A BIT O' BLARNEY.

ACT I.

SCENE. — *Glen Blarney by moonlight. Full stage. Rocky back. Rock run off* L. 3 E. *Wood and rock wings,* R. *and* L. *Set tree,* R. C. *Bushes extending out on stage for three feet* R. 2 E. *Grass couch before tree,* R. C. *Lights down. Music, " Rocky road to Dublin, O."* *Music stops as* SHEVAUN *and* DARBEY DARNEY *enter* R. 2 E. ; *each carries a whiskey keg.*

DARBEY (*grunting*). Ugh ! me legs are thremblin' undher me intirely.

SHEVAUN. Lave down yer darlin' and rist. (*Setting keg,* C.) Ugh ! (*Sits hastily.*)

DARBEY. Faix thin, I will that ! (*Sets keg down* L. C.) No ! (*Sets keg* C., *near* SHEVAUN'S.) There ! that's betther. (*Seats himself.*)

SHEVAUN. Ah, Darbey, ye're the divil, dhrunk or sober ! Well, the boys'll have plinty of whiskey for to dhrink to-morrow.

DARBEY. Thrue for ye. Sure, if they drink all the poteen in these kegs, they'll celebrate May Day in fine shtyle be raisin ructions.

SHEVAUN. Sure, like Christmas, May Day comes but wanst a year, and when it comes —

DARBEY (*interrupting*). It brings good cheer — whoo ! (*Pulls his keg up close to* SHEVAUN.)

SHEVAUN (*with pretended embarrassment*). Darbey, is it coortin' me ye are ?

DARBEY. Egorra, maybe I am ! Ah, Shevaun acushla, though I'm ould, sure me heart is as gay as the tunes of me ould fiddle.

SHEVAUN. Faith, I believe ye, Darbey, or you wouldn't be sittin' on top of a keg of the craychure in the glen at this hour o' the evenin', settin' yer caubeen for a dacint widdy like meself.

DARBEY. Shevaun acree, I don't mind tellin' ye betune ourselves here that we'd make a mighty fine pair. Sure, you could set the hearts of your cushtomers afire be sellin' a dacint drop of the craychure, an' I'd set their sowls ablaze wid the fire of me fiddle.

SHEVAUN. Thrue for ye. I niver thought o' that! Ah, Darbey, darlin', if it was not for the mimory of ould Jack in his grave this blessed night —

DARBEY. Jack is dead — long life to him! Tare an ages, Shevaun, sure ye're not goin' to tie your heart-strings forever to a tombstone?

SHEVAUN. Before he died, ten long years ago, I tould him that I'd be as thrue as a gravestone to his mimory.

DARBEY. Oh, wirra! Shevaun, sure it's me heart ye're breakin'. Bad cess to the ghost of the gravestone that's standing betune me and the colleen I love!

SHEVAUN (*bashfully*). Oh! ye'll make me blush!

DARBEY. Whisper hither a minute, Shevaun. (*She turns towards him; he snatches a kiss; noise outside,* R.)

SHEVAUN (*jumping up*). Oh! whist! (*Looking around.*) What was that?

DARBEY (*comically sentimental*). 'Twas the noise of me heart, thryin' to lep out of me mouth.

SHEVAUN (*looking* L. I E). Murdher alive! It's the gauger! He's looking for Murty Moriarty's still.

DARBEY. The divil a gauger! Maybe it's some *engagers* — some boys and their colleens, maybe, eh?

SHEVAUN. Niver mind; they'd betther not see us here wid the poteen. 'Twould hurt our kiractors, and maybe Father Murphy would make a howly show of us next Sunday from the altar! Come along, Darbey darling.

(*Exit* SHEVAUN, *carrying keg*, L. 2 E.)

DARBEY (*coming forward,* L.). Darlin'! Be the ghost of Julius Cæsar, I'm in love — wid a widdy — ohone!

(*He starts to exit,* L. I E., *when enter* TEDDY BURKE, L. I E. *They run into each other and start back.*)

TEDDY. Ough! Murther and moonlight! I see stars.

DARBEY. Av coorse ye do! Shure they're raisin' the divil up there in the sky.

TEDDY (*surprised*). What! ould Darbey Darney!

DARBEY. *Young* Darbey Darney, if ye plaze. Ould indeed! Is that Teddy Burke?

TEDDY. The divil a one else! Shure yer whiskey nearly floored me!

DARBEY (*setting it down*). Faix, it floored many a betther man.

TEDDY. Thrue for ye, Darbey! It's as bad as the shillalagh in lavin' men stretched out on the broad o' their backs.

DARBEY. What brings ye here at this hour o' the night.

TEDDY. Me two legs.

DARBEY. Teddy, acree, don't be jokin' at the expense of a gossoon like meself.

TEDDY. Darbey, they tell me ye're in love wid a widdy — Shevaun Jack!

DARBEY. For the love o' Heaven! Whist! She'll hear ye!

TEDDY. Is she here? Oh, ye vagabone! Darbey, ye're the divil!

SHEVAUN (*outside*). Darbey, ohoo!

DARBEY (*taking up keg*). Murdher! Me stayin' away is killin' her; shure she can't lave me out of her sight a minute.

TEDDY. Darbey, ye're the divil wid the girls. Sure there is not a colleen in the county that wouldn't wear out her brogues and walk miles to hear ye play the fiddle.

DARBEY (*with comic pride*). Oh, I'm a great gossoon intirely!

TEDDY. Darbey, did ye know that I was going to Amerikay?

DARBEY. Faix, no wonder. Shure yer new master is from that great country where they find the bright gold on the streets. Mr. Lawton, I mane. Tell me, Teddy acree, why is he here at all? Eh?

TEDDY. Ax me no questions and I'll tell ye no lies.

DARBEY. Mr. Lawton is a —

TEDDY. Whist! he may hear ye.

DARBEY. Why! Is he in the glen?

TEDDY. No; but I expect him here every minute. He's going up to Cork to-night, and he wants to go to Blarney Castle first, and bring away a little bit of the Blarney stone wid him. It's a quare fancy. I'm to meet him here, and take him to the castle.

SHEVAUN (*faintly, outside*). D-a-r-b-y!

DARBEY (*loudly*). Yis, darlin'! Well, Teddy, I must go. Be sure an' be at the dance at Shevaun's sheebeen to-morrow night, and we'll rise the divil out o' the May Day. *Oidhe maith leathe!* (Good-night.)

TEDDY. The top of the evenin' to you, Darbey, and may yer love for Shevaun be as strong and lasting as her whiskey!

(*Exit* DARBEY, L 2. E.)

TEDDY. Ah, wissha, Darbey Darney, ye're a caution. If ye lived to the age of Methusalem, ye'd never grow a day older than ye wor when ye wor a gossoon. Faix, it's time Misther Lawton was here. He come all the way from Amerikay to settle the ould Rossmore estates. That blaguard o' a squire is in possession now, but it takes a Yankee to take the divil be the tail, and make him screech blue murdher and brimstone. Ah, there he is now.

LAWTON (*outside* R. I E.). Teddy, ahoy!

TEDDY (*looking back* R. I E.). This way, Misther Lawton. Blarney Castle is only a little ways from here. We'll be there in a minute. Ye can see it from here be the moonlight.

LAWTON (*outside*, R. I E.). Curse this bog-hole!

(*Enter* LAWTON, R. I E.)

TEDDY.   Bog-hole! The divil a bog-hole ye'll find in a place like this.   Sure this is Glen Blarney.

LAWTON (*looking around*).   A strange place, and, by jove! a charming place.   The home of the Irish fairies, I suppose.   Eh?

TEDDY.   Faix, sor, if purty colleens and their lads are fairies, it is; for sure it's here they meet and make love to aich other.

LAWTON.   How romantic!   (*Noise of a horse galloping outside* R.)   Hello!   (*Looks* R.)   Teddy, who is that lovely looking creature on horseback dashing up the road yonder ?

TEDDY.   I may surprise ye by tellin' ye that she is Rody the Rover's own sister, fine Lady Patrice.   She lives with her cousin, Squire Rossmore, at the Blarney House.   She was brought up altogether different from her brother Rody.

LAWTON.   What a graceful rider !   (*Alarmed.*)   Hello! why the horse is running away with her !   See !

TEDDY.   Begorra, ye're right !   Yes !   (*Starts to go* R.)   Lave me shtop him !

LAWTON.   No ! No !   I wouldn't miss this chance for an adventure for a million.   Go along, Teddy.   I'll join you later.   Here is a romance !   (*Aloud.*)   Stop!   Stop!   (*Exit* LAWTON *quickly.* R. I E.)

TEDDY (*looking after him*).   Lady Patrice has lost her control, and Misther Lawton has lost his head.   Sure no wonder.   She's a beautiful lady, and maybe it's in love he'll be after fallin' wid her.   (*Looking* R.)   What !   (*Noise stops.*)   The horse is stopped ! Of course he'd stop it.   Good !   Well, he's spakin' to her.   And the Lord have mercy on him, for his heart is in the *kishoge* of her charms already.   He's taking her off the horse.   Sure she's not hurt.   Murdher and moonlight !   she's smiling at him !   Here they come.   He's tying the horse to a stone.   I'm off for the Blarney ! Mister Lawton wants to get a bit of it to take to Amerikay.   If he keeps on like this, he may be takin' something else back wid him too.

(*Exit* L. 2 E. ; *enter* LAWTON *and* PATRICE, R. I E.)

LAWTON (*leading her to couch* R. C.).   Won't you be seated? You are a trifle pale : but it is all over now.

PATRICE (*seating herself on bank*).   Thank you ; it has passed. There !

LAWTON.   I am glad.

PATRICE.   May I ask, if it is not an impertinent question, whom have I the pleasure of thanking for my fortunate escape ?

LAWTON.   Before I can answer you I must know have I had the pleasure of saving you from an accident, Lady Patrice ?

PATRICE.   Yes.

LAWTON.   Rody's sister ?

PATRICE. Yes, Rody is my brother by nature and blood, but our environment since childhood has been so different that we are more like strangers than brother and sister.

LAWTON (C.). I am sorry.

PATRICE. Not more so than I. I hope the day may not be far off when Rody, by proper and legal means, may take his position as Squire of these demesnes, and his proper place by his sister's side.

LAWTON. Rest assured that day is not far off. My name is Edward Lawton. I am an American. I have come all the way from California.

PATRICE. My uncle, who owned this estate, died in California.

LAWTON. Yes, and he left a will of which I am the sole executor.

PATRICE. You?

LAWTON. Yes. Prior to his death I was his counsel. As I said, he left a will, and that will is in my possession even now. (*Takes out a little black box.*) It is in this box. Before he expired, far away in that distant land, I sat beside his bed. (*Takes out will.*) He affixed his signature to this will, and said, "I want you, Lawton, to go to that old land of mine — old, but ever young" — and the tears filled his eyes as the memory of the old place came back to him. "Go," said he, "and under the shadow of the Blarney Castle you'll find a boy — a boy after my own heart — full of smiles and sunshine — fond of the air of his native hillsides — fond of the dance — the whip — the horses — the hounds — the hunt — fond of everything that is dear to the heart of the true Irishman! That boy," said the old Squire, "lives there. That boy shall inherit the old home of his ancestors;" and the old man's eyes lit up with pride as he asked for the will. He signed his name — and that signature makes your brother, Rody the Rover, lord of this estate!

PATRICE (*rising*). Heaven be praised! Oh, happiness! (*To* LAWTON.) You will pardon my enthusiasm. Like our dried turf, our Irish hearts burn quickly.

LAWTON. And warmly. (*Puts will in his inside pocket.*)

PATRICE. Will you walk with me as far as the house?

LAWTON. With pleasure; but only to the gate. I am going to Cork this evening. I intend visiting the Blarney before I go.

PATRICE (*going* R. 3 E). Do you intend to kiss it?

LAWTON. More. I intend stealing a piece of it so that I may be always able to kiss on occasions similar to this. (*Takes her arm.*)

PATRICE. Oh, you must have kissed it already.

LAWTON. No; the Blarney is contagious, and I must have caught it from your brother Rody. (*Exeunt* R. 3 E.)

(Pause; Music, "Rocky Road to Dublin." Enter RODY THE
ROVER, L. 3 E.)

RODY. Well, I'm here. I fell ashleep in ould Shevaun's shebeen this afthernoon, an' only for the salt ould Shevaun put on
me face, I'd be ashleep yet, an' miss my little Rosaleen. Bad
luck to me, I thought I saw a fairy. I thought I was on me
way here, and while passing by the ould *rath*,* who the divil should
lep up afore me on the boreen but a little craychure abou*t*
the size of me small finger. And the two eyes he set on me !
Be the mug of Mathusalem ! I thought I was bewitched ! There
the little spalpeen stood, looking up at me overright me two eyes
out. Me little buccho wore a cap like a butther cup, an' a lither
apron, and (like the Scotchman) the divil a pair of breeches had
he on at all. Sure he had a nose as red as Cuddeen Cassidy's
hair, and it stuck out as sharp and pinted as the thorn o' me
shillalagh. We looked at aich other. The divil a word he said
to me, and, faix, I said the same to him. Afther awhile — " Good-
mornin'," sez I, be the way of introduction, tho' it was the afternoon.
" The top of the mornin'," sez he, wid a rich Tipperary brogue.
His voice ! Murdher ! I wish I had a photograph of it. " Who
are ye ?" sez I. " The Leprehaun," sez he. " The Leprehaun?"
sez I again, like that. " Yis," sez he. Faix ! I was surprised.
" The Leprehaun ? " sez I again. " The divil a wan else," sez he.
" Murdher and turf ! Rody, the Rover, ye're a rich man," sez I ;
for I knew that if I caught the Leprehaun he'd give me a pot of
goold to lave him go. " Come here, ye thief of the world," sez I ;
and with that I made a grab for him. Whish ! What do you
think, but the little vagabone threw a handful of salt in my eyes.
" Holy Moses and murdher !" I screeched ; and with that I woke
up, and there was me lady Shevaun throwin' salt in me face,
thryin' to wake me up. Sure, I wuz layin' undher the table in her
shebeen, drunk. Ahem ! I mane dramin'. " Rody, ye vagabone," sez I, " ye'd betther be startin' for the glen, or Rosaleen
will raise the divil wid ye," and wid that I ran out and didn't shtop
a step till I came here. (*Enter*. LAWTON, R. 3 E.) Ah, Misther
Lawton.

LAWTON. Hello! Rody! you here!
RODY. Don't ye see I am ; bad luck to me !
LAWTON. What the deuce brings you here ?
RODY. Me legs, bad scran to them !
LAWTON (R.). Rody, I think I can guess, — a charming little
colleen perhaps ? Eh ?
RODY. Faix, ye hit it that time, as the bull said to the butcher.
LAWTON. Tell me about her, is she pretty?
RODY. Ah, sor, sure she's got a pair of eyes as bright as the
buckles of me new shoes, and a mouth l:ke a burstin' rose, that
blarneyizes ye wid its sweetness.

* NOTE. — A burying ground for infants who die before baptism.

LAWTON. And her heart —

RODY. Her heart! Faix, it's as warm an' as dear as a noggin of Shevaun Jack's whiskey! And her feet! Sure she has two of the purtiest bits of poetry in shoe leather ye ever set your eyes upon. Sure, sor, she's a little flower that grew on an Irish hillside and wuz brought up ateing and dhrinking the divil a thing but sweet dew and sunlight.

LAWTON. And the name of your flower is —

RODY. Rosaleen — manin' a little rose. (*Spoken through music.*) She is a poor orphan, sor. Her mother died. Sure when the black throuble kem upon her, sure I thought I'd lose her. Me purty flower began to fade — the bright color left its leaves, and 'twas white they was gettin' for the want of the sunlight. The light of my heart fell upon it and brought it back to life agin, and now me heart is brimmin' over wid happiness, and sure the whole world looks smilin' and goolden in the light of our true love. (*Stop music.*)

LAWTON. Ah, Rody, I am glad that I'm to be the means of completely filling your cup of happiness.

RODY. Ye mane that will? Then it is for me? I am the owner of the Rossmore estates?

LAWTON. That I won't say yet. The contents of that will are sacred until I return from Cork next week, whither I am going to make my final arrangements toward the settlement of this estate. Rody, I'm going to Blarney before I take the nine o'clock train for Cork. I want to get a bit of the stone for a curiosity. (*Looks at watch.*) It is now half-past eight — I'll have time to do it. Won't you come as far as the castle with me?

RODY. Certainly, sor. I can't go far as I'm expectin' Rosaleen.

(*Exeunt* L. 3 E.)

(*Pause.* ROSALEEN *is heard singing* "The Groves of Blarney" *outside* R. 1 E. *She enters singing the last line.*)

ROSALEEN. The Groves of Blarney! Wissha! may the Lord presarve them and keep thim foriver green like the mimory of the oulden time, when the castle beyant was in all its glory! Blarney Castle! The place where all the purtiest things ever whispered in the ear of a colleen are stowed away. Ah, may the ould stone never grow mossy for the want of a kiss! Sure there isn't a purtier place in the whole world for coortin' than under its kindly shadow. An' it's here where I'm to meet my rovin' Rody to-night. My Rody! My Rover! The finest bit of manhood in the whole of Munster, much less the County Cork.

(*Enter* CUDDEEN CASSIDY, L. 2 E.)

Is that you, Rody?

CUDDEEN. No, it isn't that rovin' vagabone, but no less a person than Misther Cuddeen Cassidy, a dacint respectable man.

ROSALEEN. Misther Cassidy is the only man in the county that thinks so.

CUDDEEN. Ye'd better keep a civil tongue in yer head until ye're sure you're right. Faith, there is more people in the county than meself that thinks so.

ROSALEEN. That's all. They only think so, but they don't know.

CUDDEEN. There's me fine Squire Rossmore, for example, eh?

ROSALEEN (C.). A bird of your own kind; but he's got finer feathers.

CUDDEEN. Ye're not paying the Squire any fine compliments, Rosaleen, alanna. It isn't for you to say mane things agin the Squire —

ROSALEEN (*interrupting*). Oh, thin I'm saying mane things agin the Squire when I'm comparin' him to yerself. I thought Misther Cassidy, Esquire (*sarcastically*) was a dacint respectable gentleman. Eh? Cuddeen?

CUDDEEN. Ah, Rosaleen, darlin', ye've got the gift of gab, and ye're thrying to be sarcasticating wid an old craychure like meself. Sure it was a kind mother for ye to have a smart tongue.

ROSALEEN. Cuddeen! Shtop! Nivir agin let me hear that tongue of yers spake the name of me poor mother, who is dead in her grave this blessed night (Lord have mercy on her soul!).

CUDDEEN. May she rest in pace. I'm sure it wouldn't be for the likes o' me to be takin' the dead out of their graves this blessed night.

ROSALEEN. Well, Cuddeen — or Misther Cassidy, indeed, if ye have anything to say to me I wish ye'd say it, and not keep me here talking agin' me will.

CUDDEEN. Oh, the divil a word I have to say at all, at all! (*Shrewdly.*) Only that Squire Maurice thinks enough of me to confide a purty little sacret in my ear.

ROSALEEN. Ye don't tell me so?

CUDDEEN. Yis, an' sure only for it's a sacret I wouldn't be after telling it to ye.

ROSALEEN. Indeed! An' ye wouldn't tell me only for it's a sacret.

CUDDEEN. No. (*Drawing near her.*) Whisper hither a minute. No less a gentleman than Squire Maurice himself is in love wid ye.

ROSALEEN. Is that so? We hear ducks! Sure I thought he was in love with Rody's sister, Lady Patrice.

CUDDEEN. Faix, no, she wouldn't give a traneen for his soul and body, for she nivir liked him.

ROSALEEN. An' it's me that he is in love with, eh?

CUDDEEN. Yis; the apple bloom in yer cheeks, and the light o' the sky in yer Irish eyes, and yer purty instep plazes Squire's fancy, and it's mistress of the Blarney house he'd be makin' ye if ye'd only consent to consider —

ROSALEEN (*interrupting*). Stop, ye blaguard! or I'll twist the
tongue out of yer wicked ould head!

(*Enter* RODY, R. 3 E.)

RODY (*coming down run aside*). The blackbird and the dove!
(*He listens at* C. *in rear, unobserved.*)
CUDDEEN (*to* ROSALEEN). I see. It's in love wid that divil-
may-care spalpeen ye are. - That wandering thief of the world that
niver did a shtroke of a day's work in his life.
ROSALEEN. You mane Rody?
CUDDEEN. Yis, the Rover! The gintleman that never did —
ROSALEEN (*interrupting*). The gentleman that never chated
his people out of their money and manes. The gentleman who
was too honest-hearted to stale, and too good to lie. No! He
left yer fine Squire Maurice to do that. Rody respected the mimory of his uncle too much to grab the land even before he was sure
that the ould Squire was dead.
CUDDEEN. Well, what's the manin' of all this?
ROSALEEN. It manes that I love Rody, and that I hate his
cousin, the Squireen! Ye may tell him from me that rather than
wear his silks an' satins, in ragged petticoats I'd walk barefooted
from Cape Clear to the Giant's Causeway; for I love Rody the
Rover with all my heart.
RODY (*springing forward*, C.). And Rody loves Rosaleen with
his whole heart and soul (*clasps her*), and would cling to her even
if the whole world tried to drag her away! (*Chord.*)
CUDDEEN (L.; *astonished*). Rody!
RODY. Yis — the rover. (*Imitating* CUDDEEN'S *voice.*) "That
wandherin' thief o' the world, that niver did a shtroke o' a day's
work in his life."
CUDDEEN. When ye spake of the divil, he usually appears.
RODY. Yis; we were talking about *you* to-night.
CUDDEEN. I thought me ears were burnin'.
RODY. It would be a mighty fine thing for the village if they
were burned off intirely. And mind ye, if ye don't lave me sight,
I'll be timpted to burn some other part of ye, and use the top o'
me shoe for a match.
CUDDEEN. Ye don't like me, Rody, eh?
RODY. For a short answer — no. Words are too sweet to
waste on the likes of ye.
CUDDEEN. Ye're sharp wid yer tongue.
RODY. I wish to Heaven I was sharper, so that I could cut yer
company quicker. (*Coming forward* C.) Cuddeen Cassidy, take
a fool's advice and lave this spot.
CUDDEEN. Lave this spot, is it? It should be *you* that should
be *lavin* it. Ye're on yer cousin's land. Squire Maurice owns
this bit o' ground, an' I work for him.
RODY. He won't own it long, with the blessin' o' Heaven.

CUDDEEN. How do ye know?

RODY. Listen, an' I'll tell ye somethin' that'll shrivel up your heart like a roasted cockel, and put the goose-flesh on yer sowl.

ROSALEEN. Out wid it, Rody.

RODY (*to* CUDDEEN). Listen, then. When me uncle died in Amerikay, he left a will.

CUDDEEN. Are ye sure o' that?

RODY. Yis. Do ye know the stranger that arrived in the village yesterday from America?

CUDDEEN. Yis; Mr. Lawton. What has he got to do wid it?

RODY. He was me uncle's lawyer in California. He came over wid a will to settle the Irish estates; and, wid Heaven's help, we'll know next week whether the Squireen or meself owns this land.

CUDDEEN (*aside*). Whew! there'll be blood on the moon an' music in the wind! (*To* RODY.) But tell me, Rody, are ye sure that the will is favorable to yer good?

RODY. I mane to make sure. I mane to get that will, and prove that I was the boy me uncle loved — a rover like himself. 'Tis to me he'd lave the land, and not to the likes of your master.

CUDDEEN. Thim's hard words agin' the Squire. Worse could be said agin yerself.

RODY. What d'ye mane?

CUDDEEN. That a dacint gossoon niver, unbeknownst to the priest, meets a purty colleen in this lonely glen after night.

ROSALEEN. O Rody!

RODY (*stepping* C.). Tut! Take that! (*Strikes* CUDDEEN *in the face and fells him.*) An' if it wasn't for the presence of that same colleen. I'd put me hand down yer throat and tear out yer black tongue for saying so.

ROSALEEN. O Rody, darlin', lave him alone! It's in jail he'll be after puttin' ye.

RODY. It's there he belongs. (*To* CUDDEEN.) Get up. ye slanderous rapscallion, or I'll flail ye alive wid this shillalah that's itching to dance a jig on the seat of yer breeches.

CUDDEEN. Ough, murdher — me phizoge! Sweet bad luck to ye. Believe me, me fine bouchaloge, that blow will cost ye trouble — that poultoge will bring the bitterness to yer heart, and blind wid tears the bright eyes of that colleen there. Rody, mark my words, that poultoge will be paid back, and wid compound interest. The Cassidys have the black blood in their veins, and they never forgive an enemy or forget an injury.

(*Exit* L. 1 E.)

RODY (L., *after him*). Oh, ho! We hear drakes, as the duck said.

ROSALEEN (C.). O Rody, darlin'! I'm afraid, wirra; I have a presintiment that his words will come true.

RODY. Nivir fear, mavourneen. Sure he was talking throu'h his caubeen that time. (*Indicating bank* R. C.) Sit down, aroon, and don't be superstitious (ROSALEEN *seats herself* R. C.) Superstition is the great curse of our country, and the sooner we get rid of it the better. Look at me, for instance, a rovin', harum-scarum son of the ould sod, that doesn't care a divil for peelers or goats, egorra, or even Cassidys. No, darlin', cheer up. Keep a warm heart in yer bosom, for soon we'll both be happy. (*Music.*)

ROSALEEN. Shake some of those furze blossoms on me, darlin'.

RODY (*shaking furze-bush; bus.*). Sure I will, mavourneen, for they're as golden as yer own lovely hair, and as sweet as yer purty lips. (*Kisses her while blossoms are falling.*) There's a smack o' the Blarney for ye. (*Throws himself at her feet.*)

ROSALEEN. O Rody!

RODY. Sure, the furze-bush, darlin', is like the life we live, — it is purty an' bloomin', but sure the thorns and the throubles are on it, as the pig said when he wanted to ate the porcupine.

ROSALEEN. O Rody, sure it's happy I am this night!

RODY. Ah, aroon, sure, to hear ye say that is sweeter to me senses than the scint o' the shamrocks. Tell me agin, Rosaleen, that ye love me! Sure, it sends the drops o' joy into me eyes, and me heart seems as if it would burst wid happiness.

ROSALEEN (*flinging her arms about his neck*). Rody, I love you.

RODY (*joyfully*). Ah, acushla, that sentence is sweeter to me than the bag-pipes! Sweeter music to me sowl than the harp or the fiddle! Ah, light o' me heart, sure 'tis happy ye've made me! Rosaleen, mavourneen, I love ye, too. Sure, ye're a little angel o' love that dropped down from heaven an' made yer home in me heart.

ROSALEEN. O Rody, sure it's a poet ye are.

RODY. The divil a lie for ye, darlin'. (*Looking up.*) Look at the moon up there; sure, she's laughing at us. An' no wonder! She's been listening to the same ould shtory ever since Adam and Eve set the fashion.

ROSALEEN. Ah, Rody, your sweet love was the sunshine that drove the clouds from my heart. When me poor mother died, sure 'twas your love that filled the empty place in my heart, and brought me comfort and consolation.

RODY. An' may it always, darlin'. (*Kisses her.*) Then another smack o' the Blarney for yer purty lips.

ROSALEEN. O Rody, I'm as happy as a little flower when it's kissed by the sunlight.

RODY. Sure, it's small wonder we're happy. Here we are, lovin' in the moonlight, and the purty stars winking at us overhead, and the sleeping flowers. like the incense at the chapel, are flinging their fragrance at us. (*Sings verse from " Molly Bawn."*)

> Sure, the purty flowers were made to grow, love,
> And the purty stars were made to shine;
> And maybe I was made for you, love,
> And maybe you were made for mine.

(*Speaking.*) How d'ye like that, me jewel?

ROSALEEN. Sure, it goes to me heart like a bit o' music. Won't you sing a song, Rody, to plaze me? Do! Sure, yer voice is as sweet to me ears as Father Murphy's mass bell.

RODY (*rising*). I'll sing for ye, mavourneen. (*Gives her his stick.*) Rest me shillalah, then, agin the tree, an' I'll sing about yerself, wid yer lovely hair and shining blue eyes.

ROSALEEN. Ah, Rody, it's Blarney Castle that's botherin' ye. Sure, 'tis the Blarney ye're giving me.

RODY. Faix, no. I'm giving ye "Sweet Rosaleen." (*Music; sings. Any other song may be substituted.*)

Oh, I love a purty colleen!
Her name it is sweet Rosaleen,
And she lives beside the Blarney, where the flowers grow bright;
Wid golden hair and lovely eyes,
Reflectin' the light of the skies,
An' shamin' wid their brightness the stars at night!

O Rosaleen!
Sweet Rosaleen!
Pulse o' me heart — my Irish queen!
My lovely little Rosaleen,
My own Colleen!

Sure, she's singing in the mornin',
When the dew-dhrops are adornin'
The purty little posies wid the jewels so bright;
She's smilin' in the afternoon,
As sunny as a day in June,
And laughing in the evening, an' loving at night.

O Rosaleen!
Sweet Rosaleen!
Pulse o' my neart — my Irish queen!
My lovely little Rosaleen,
My own Colleen!

When the stars above are peepin',
And the little birds are sleepin',
It is then that I am thinking of my own Colleen,
Whose warm heart and sunny smile
All care and trouble can beguile.
Sure, there isn't a girl in Munster like sweet Rosaleen!

(ROSALEEN *rises.*)

O Rosaleen!
(*Puts arm around her waist.*)
Sweet Rosaleen!
Pulse o' me heart — my Irish queen!
(*Starts to go.* L. 2 E.)
My lovely little Rosaleen,
My own Colleen!

(*Exeunt* L. 2 E.; RODY *leaves his stick behind him; enter* SQUIRE ROSSMORE, R. 2 E.)

SQUIRE (*looking after them*). Hello! there she is, the loveliest creature in the village, an' with that useless vagrant, that scapegrace of the family. By Jove! she's a wild-flower — as sweet and beautiful as a rose on an Irish hillside. I should like to put that wild-flower near my heart. Ah, well. one can do many things if they but try. (*Looks around.*) It is quiet here. This glen is a charming old spot. It would transform a jackass into a poet. (*Lighting his cigar.*) With a quietude like this, óne can't help thinking. (*Throwing himself on bank.*) I wonder what the devil that mysterious American is doing in this village. He seems to be an interesting sort of a chap. I might invite him to supper at the Blarney House, but these Americans are so deucedly Democratic in their ideas that they cannot comprehend the conception of class and quality. (*Hears noise.*) Hello! (*Loudly; looking* L. 1 E.) Who's there?

(*Enter* CUDDEEN, L. 1 E.)

CUDDEEN. Only yer shadow in the person of meself.
SQUIRE. Oh! Cassidy; come here. I wish to speak with you. (CASSIDY *crosses to* R.) Cassidy, the villagers say that you know everything.
CUDDEEN. I have that character, sor, — thanks to yer cousin Rody for it.
SQUIRE. I'll put your powers to the proof. Can you tell me who is that American who frequents the village at present?
CUDDEEN. Ye mane the man that tuk Teddy Burke for his servant?
SQUIRE. Yes.
CUDDEEN. That's a Misther Lawton, and he came from Amerikay out in California. They say that he was the ould Squire's lawyer out there.
SQUIRE (*surprised*). My uncle's? Eh?
CUDDEEN. Yis. They do be saying that yer uncle left a will when he died. This man manes to prove, I think, that your cousin Rody is the thrue heir to this property.
SQUIRE (*rising*). What! Are you sure of that?
CUDDEEN. I have Rody's own word for it.
SQUIRE. You are sure, you say?
CUDDEEN. For certain; as sure as me name is Cuddeen Cassidy.
SQUIRE. Rody, my cousin, must never get that will.
CUDDEEN. Faix, he says that he manes to get it.
SQUIRE (*crossing to* L. C. *front*). But I say that he shall not.
CUDDEEN (*crossing to* C.). Good! More power to your resolves!
SQUIRE. Where is this American to be found?
CUDDEEN. He's stopping at Father Murphy's. I heard Father Murphy's sister say that he was going to Cork to-night, and that he'd be back agin next week.
SQUIRE. I might invite him to the Blarney House. Cassidy, you are a connoisseur on mixed drinks — you might fix some wine for him.
CUDDEEN (*aside*). Ye vagabone!
SQUIRE. No; on second thought, 'twere best I should not see him.

CUDDEEN. Ye mane for me to see him, eh? Are ye to consider yerself a monkey, and Cuddeen Cassidy a cat wid a quick paw? (*Crosses to* R.) Oh, no, no!

SQUIRE (*crosses to* C.). Cassidy, your mother is dying in the poorhouse.

CUDDEEN. Yis — more shame to me for it!

SQUIRE. At what do you value her life?

CUDDEEN. Value it? It's above pricin'.

SQUIRE. Not at all. That will. Would you like to extricate your mother and yourself from the grasp of poverty?

CUDDEEN (*getting excited*). What! Do you mane it?

SQUIRE. Yes.

CUDDEEN (*excitedly*). You'll take me poor mother out of the poorhouse? You'll do that? You'll give her plenty to ate and drink? You'll do all that? Do, and I'll go through fire for ye! I'll do anything! Look! Me hands are strong! Me muscles are as firm as steel! The fire of despair is in me heart! O Squire, agra, you'll save me mother from a pauper's grave? Do that, an' I'll see that Rody'll never get that will. I'll bring it to *you* — to *you*. I'll stale — rob — kill — no! no! not murdher. Me hands would be red wid blood, and I could never stretch them out to welcome me old mother back.

SQUIRE, I'll do it all! On my honor!

CUDDEEN. Honor? Whist! If ye had any ye wouldn't be trying to chate yer own cousin out o' his birthright.

SQUIRE. Cassidy!

CUDDEEN. I ax yer pardon. But never fear, I'll keep me word. I'll get that will. An' listen: if ye go back on yer word — mind ye, now, you'll curse the mother and father that brought you to this world — this world that has no heart or sowl. (*Noise heard.*)

SQUIRE. Hush! What's that?

CUDDEEN (*listening*). What?

SQUIRE (*looking* L.). Somebody coming down the road from the castle.

CUDDEEN (*crossing to* L.). Whist! Look! It's Mr. Lawton, the American, and Teddy Burke; they've been at the Blarney Castle.

SQUIRE. Then I'm off. Good-night. (*Starting to go* R. 3 E.)

CUDDEEN. Is it laving me alone ye are? (*Aside.*) The coward! (*Aloud.*) Nivir fear; Cuddeen Cassidy is no coward. He will get that will, even if it was hidden behind the altar in Father Murphy's chapel.

SQUIRE. If you get it, hide it for a few days; then bring it to me. Good-night. (*Exit* SQUIRE, R. 3 E.)

CUDDEEN. If I get it, I'll keep it until the robbery blows over, like a nine days' wonder. When the promise is made good, then the Squire may have it and welcome. Whist! They're coming this way. I'll hide behind the rock here. (*Exit*, R. 2 E.)

(*Enter* LAWTON, *followed by* TEDDY BURKE, L. 3 E.)

LAWTON. You need not come any farther, Teddy. Well, Blarney Castle is certainly interesting. Oh, you Irish people are so fond of moss-covered traditions. By jingo! Your imagination is the strongest part of you.

TEDDY. Our only fault, sor, is that our hearts are bigger than our heads.

LAWTON. In our country we change all that; we pay more attention to the head.

TEDDY. At the expense of the heart, sor — I'm sorry.

LAWTON. Oh, we develop both equally. You see that gives us a moral equilibrium.

TEDDY. I niver saw one, sor.

LAWTON (*laughing*). I see, Teddy, you don't quite comprehend. (*Looking at watch.*) But I must go. I have just three minutes to catch the Cork train.

TEDDY. The station isn't a minute's walk, sor. Cut across the Squire's field, there. (*Points* R.)

LAWTON. The Squire's?

TEDDY. I mane Squire Rody's field.

LAWTON. Now you speak the truth. Here, Teddy, you had better take this box and bring it back to Father Murphy's. (*Gives box.*) I would not lose what it contains for the world. It is priceless. Take good care of it.

TEDDY. Oh, niver fear, sor. I'll guard it as if it were me own life.

(*Re-enter, partially*, CUDDEEN.)

CUDDEEN (*aside*). It's in that box. I'll get it or die. (*Exit.*)

LAWTON (*aside*). I've got the will in my pocket; only a bit of the Blarney stone is in the box. It is just as well to let Teddy think that it contains the will. He will guard it better. (*Aloud.*) Teddy, I am making you custodian of that box to test your good qualities. If you prove trustworthy, I'll take you back to America with me.

TEDDY. Oh, niver fear, sor; this box is as safe as if St. Patrick himself had his two fingers on it.

LAWTON. Now I must start for the train.

TEDDY. Begorra, like a sneeze, it won't wait.

LAWTON. Good-by, Teddy; I'll be back in a week. You left my luggage at the station?

TEDDY. Yis, sor.

LAWTON. And remember — take good care of that box until I return. *Au revoir!*

(*Exit* LAWTON, R. 3 E; *gradually lower lights until it is quite dark.*)

TEDDY. Over the water, sor. (*Aside*.) Ah, I have Rody's happiness too much to heart to lave anything happen to this box. Ah, that's a thrue American gintleman. He slipped a half crown into me hand jist now for no other reason than that I risked the crown of me head in tryin' to knock off a bit o' the famous Blarney stone beyant, whilst he held me be the two legs. He took it to Cork wid him, and like a gintleman he laves me to take care o' the box wid the will. (*Dramatic music till the end of act. Re-enter* CUDDEEN *unobserved; he stealthily crawls up behind* TEDDY *and gets possession of* RODY'S *stick, which is lying on bank* R. C.) Well, he won't be sorry, for I'll guard it wid me life. The moon is getting clouded; it'll be dark soon. I'd better be startin' back wid me little box. Whew! It's dark. (*By this time* CUDDEEN *has crossed to* L. *in front;* TEDDY *sees him and starts back. Chord.*) The Lord betune us an' all harm! Who's that?

CUDDEEN (*with determination*). Give up that box. Give it up, I'm tellin' ye.

TEDDY. Go to the divil! Faith, I believe ye are the divil. (*Boldly.*) Who are ye?

CUDDEEN. A despairin' man that wants that box.

TEDDY (*clutching box tighter*). He'll niver git it while Teddy Burke has his hands on it.

CUDDEEN (*striking him with stick*). Take that, an' see if it will waken your hould any.

TEDDY. Oh, help! help! Mr. Lawton! Police!

CUDDEEN. The police are target shootin' to-day, and haven't come back yet. Give me that box!

TEDDY. Murther! Thieves! Help! Help!

CUDDEEN (*grasping him by the throat*). Hould yer tongue, bad cess to ye! (*Strikes him on head.*) There! That may convince ye that I'm the strongest.

TEDDY. Ye coward!

CUDDEEN. There — and there! (*Strikes him twice.*)

TEDDY. Murther! I'm kilt, oh!

(*The moon comes out; lights half up.*)

TEDDY (*recognizing him*). Cuddeen Cassidy!

CUDDEEN. Whist!

TEDDY. Ye robber!

CUDDEEN. Ye lie! (*Strikes him again.*) There! (TEDDY *falls* C.) That may silence ye.

TEDDY (*on ground*). Murdherer! Ugh! God in heaven: Oh! (TEDDY *falls back dead, box still clutched in his arms; have salt ready, rear,* C.)

CUDDEEN. No, not murdherer! Whist! Wake up! Ye're not dead! Look at me! (*Listens to heart.*) Ah! it's stopped! The could feeling is stalin' on. God alive, he's dead — dead! (*Owl hoots outside.*) Whist! Some one's comin'. (*Listens.*) No, it's the hootin' o' the owls, or maybe the banshee. The red mark o' Cain is burnin' me forehead. I'm a murdherer. (*Looks at* TEDDY.) No! No! Ah, yer eyes are open! (*Lifting him up.*) Ye're not dead! I'm no murdherer! Don't look at me like that! Your eyes are wide open! (*Starts back horrified.*) Howly Mother in heaven! The light o' life has left them. It's the could stare o' the corpse that's accusing me o' murther! I've kilt him! Yes —yes — for what? The box — ah, yes, the box! (*Takes it from corpse.*) I have it. Here it is. I've paid dearly for it. It must be worth the price. Ah, shut yer eyes! You'll drive me mad — mad! (RODY *is heard singing in distance faintly* "*The pretty girl milking her cow.*" *During singing* CUDDEEN *speaks spasmodically and continues scene. As the singing draws nearer, drums are heard beating in the distance.*) What's that — the banshee singing the death-song? (*To body.*) I must hide ye where nobody'll find ye till I'm far away. (*Takes up body and drags it along.*) The furze-bushes! No, the water! The Shannon'll hide me crime! Ugh! How heavy ye are! Made o' lead. Ugh! (*Drums heard louder.*) What's that? My God! The police returning from the target shooting! I'm lost! lost! There! Ah! (*Throws body into water; throw up salt as body falls behind ground row.*) Sleep there! Your white lips are dumb! You'll never accuse me of murther! The box! (*Picks it up.*) I've got it! I must hide it! What's this? The stick! (*Picks it up.*) It's Rody the Rover's! He's coming for it! He won't get it! (*Throws it behind the rock.*) Ah, 'tis proof! Rody's the murdherer! I'm free — free! (*Goes up stage laughing hysterically and wildly; warn curtain.*)

(*Enter* RODY, L. I E., *singing last line,* "*The purty girl milking her cow.*" CUDDEEN *crouches up stage and watches him.*)

RODY. Faith, I lost me blackthorn! Sure, it's my shadow: I must find it. (*Looks around; listens.*) The drums! The police are coming back from the target shooting. Maybe I left it up here. (*Goes up stage and looks around on ground for stick.*)

(*Enter* CAPTAIN CASTLETON *and police marching,* R. I E.)

CAPTAIN CASTLETON. Halt! (*They do so. He notices* RODY'S *figure.*) What's that? (*To police.*) Be ready! A smuggler! Take aim.
RODY (*rising up* C.). Hold, for the love o' Heaven!
CASTLETON. Who are you? Answer!
CUDDEEN. He's a smuggler and a murdherer!
RODY. It's a lie. I'm a dacint boy, an' me name is Rody the Rover.

(*Tableau; light full up.*)

CURTAIN.

ACT II.

SCENE. — SHEVAUN'S *shebeen at sunset. Entrances* C. *and* R. 3 E.; *window in flat; fireplace,* R. 2 E.; *tables* R. C. *and* L. C. *Peasants seated around table* R. *at curtain rise.* DARBEY DARNEY *at table* L. *with fiddle.* RODY *at table* R., *singing* "*Cruiskeen Lawn.*"

RODY (*singing*).

> Let the farmer praise his grounds,
> As the huntsman does his hounds,
> And the shepherd his dew-scented lawn,
> While I, more blessed than they,
> Sing each happy night and day   (*Curtain.*)
> With my smiling little Cruiskeen Lawn.

(*Chorus of Peasants.*)

> Gra machree, ma cruiskeen,
> Slanta Gal mavourneen,
> Gra machra ma Cruiskeen Lawn, Lawn, Lawn.
> Agus gra ma Colleen Bawn.

(*Enter* SHEVAUN, R. 3 E.)

SHEVAUN. Be aisy wid yer singin'; it's the peelers ye'll be afther bringing down on me head this blessed day for selling an honest dhrop of the craychure.

RODY. Niver fear, Shevaun, darlint; the divil a policeman'll trouble this whiskey — faith, it's strong enough to take care of itself. Here's to your health, Shevaun, and may you live till you die; and shure, when you do die, may you be tin days in heaven before the divil reads of your death in the *London Times*.

SHEVAUN. Ah, wirra, be aisy!

RODY. Aroo, what harm is there in takin' a dhrop of poteen? Sure, boys, it sends the blood dancin' through our veins, and lights the fire o' fun in our hearts, and gives us courage to say, —

(*Sings.*)

> When grim death appears,
> After few but happy years,
> To tell me that me race has run,
> I say, begone ye knave —
> Sure our breeches gave me lave
> For to have another Cruiskeen Lawn.

(*Chorus of Peasants.*)

OMNES. Hurroo! *Iss mogh e shin.* Ah, ha, wisha. (*All drink.*) Slanta leath Rody na Rover.

RODY. Now, boys, a health to Shevaun, and may she always be as lively and shtrong as her whiskey. (*All drink.*)

SHEVAUN (*going to table* R.). Faith, I'll taste a dhrop meself to warm the cockles o' me ould heart. (*Takes glass.*) A health to the purtiest colleen that iver danced in shoeleather. She was crowned by the boys and girls this blessed May Day Queen o' the May — Rosaleen.

(*Omnes drink and scatter around.*)

DARBEY DARNEY (*rising*). Sure, me ould fiddle 'll go to ruin for want o' scrapin', if the colleens don't hurry back from the chapel. (*Loud laughter outside.*)

SHEVAUN (*going to* D. C.). Whist! Here they are as frisky as lambs in the springtime. (*Lively music; enter* ROSALEEN, *followed by girls*, C.)

RODY. *Cead mille failthe* to the whole of ye! (*Taking* ROSA-LEEN *by the hand.*) Come, Rosaleen, acushla, I want ye to help me knock the sparks out o' the floor with a rale ould Irish breakdown.

SHEVAUN. Rody, ye're the divil!

RODY. Whoo!

ROSALEEN. Come, girls, we'll give the May Day an Irish goodnight.

RODY. Darbey, ye divil, get upon the table there, an' put the resin to your bow. Whoo! (*Helps* DARBEY *upon the table.*)

DARBEY (*crawling upon the table*). Ah, thin, whin I was a gossoon in the ould times o' '48 there wasn't a colleen in the country could hould a foot wid me. (*Sadly.*) But I'm gettin' ould now.

RODY. The divil a bit! The age is only on yer hair, Darbey; the youth is still in yer heart.

DARBEY. Yes, begorra, and in me legs too? (*Dances on table; stops suddenly.*) Ough! The rumatizm is risin' the divil with me intirely. (*Seats himself in chair on table.*) Niver mind a bouchaloge. I'll knock the fire out o' me fiddle. (*Plays lively air.*)

RODY. Come, boys and girls! (*They square off for a dance.*) I'd twirl me shillalah wid ye, but I lost it somewhere last night. Whoo, ye divils, ye! (*Irish country dance; specialties; songs and dances.*)

OMNES. Hurroo! Bravo! Hurroo! Ah, ah!

SHEVAUN. Shure, it's the happy set ye're all! Sure, I wish meself were young agin.

DARBEY (*firing away fiddle and leaping from table*). Ah, fa'x, we're all young agin. Come, Shevaun, and we'll show the gaffers a dance in a rale ould shtyle. (*Music comic; dance between* SHE-VAUN *and* DARBEY.)

DARBEY (*stopping suddenly*). Ah, the rumatizm is risin' the divil wid me intirely!

(*Enter* CUDDEEN CASSIDY, C. *door.*)

CUDDEEN (*at door*). God save all here! (*Seeing* RODY, L.) Barrin' that vagabone there. (*Comes in* C.)

RODY. The divil shoot ye! (*To* SHEVAUN, R.) Shevaun, did ye want to become a blessed saint?

SHEVAUN. Heaven save us — how?

RODY. By banishing that snake there. Maybe ye'll prove yerself a second St. Patrick.

CUDDEEN (C.). Ah, Shevaun darn't tell me not to darken her door. She knows me too well, an', besides, she sells a dhrop o' the whiskey on the sly, an' it's nobody knows it better than Cuddeen Cassidy.

SHEVAUN (*going to fireplace*, R.). Murdher, the kittle is boiling over!

CUDDEEN. She darsn't turn me from her door, ye see.

SHEVAUN (*at fireplace*). Ah, a brass pinny 'd make me scald ye wid the kittle and make black tay out o' ye.

RODY. What! An' pizen the whole o' us?

DARBEY. Put him out in the pigsty with the *banives*, bad luck to him!

CUDDEEN. Keep your pusoge to yer fiddle, ye omadhaun!

DARBEY. Murdher! (*Starts for him*; RODY *holds him back.*)

RODY. Hould, Darbey — don't dirty yer hands wid him.

SHEVAUN (*crossing to* L.). Darbey, be aisy. (*Rubbing her sooty hands over his cheeks.*) Sure, I love you.

DARBEY. Sure, you'll make me blush; begorra, me cheeks are red now.

CUDDEEN. An' as for ye, Rody the Rover, ye'd better be afther buying yer passage for Amerikay to save yer neck from the rope.

RODY. What!

CUDDEEN. It's the truth I'm tellin' ye. Teddy Burke was murdhered in the glen last night.

OMNES. What!

CUDDEEN. Yes; and his body thrown into the Shannon. It was found jist now at the foot of Shlieve Bwee. Teddy Burke kept the will o' the Rossmore estate for Mr. Lawton, the American.

RODY. Well!

CUDDEEN. Well, it's gone, and you, Rody the Rover, were in the glen last night. (*Starts up stage.*)

RODY (*wildly*). Murdher and turf! Lave me at him! Ye vagabone! (*Seizes* CUDDEEN, *and throws him out of window. Crash outside.*) Get out there wid the pigs, where ye belong! (*All laugh.*)

SHEVAUN. Howly murdher! It's the peelers he'll be afther bringin' down on our heads.

RODY (*coming down stage* R.). Bad manners to him! (*To* SHE-

VAUN.) Shevaun, give me a dhrop o' water to wash me hands afther handling the spalpeen. (*Takes off coat.*)

SHEVAUN (*going to cupboard* L.). Here's some in the basin. (*Pours out water and lays dish on table* R.) There ye are. (SHE-VAUN *looks out of window.*) Murdher! The pig's tore the sate of his breeches. (RODY *washes his hands, then drys them with towel.*)

ROSALEEN (*at door, looking* L.). Oh, the bonfires are lit, an' the pipes are playin', and the lads and their colleens are dancin' on the green. (CASSIDY *pokes his dirty face in the window.* RODY *throws out water and douses him.*)

CUDDEEN. Ough! Murdher! (*Disappears.*)

(*Omnes laugh.*)

RODY. Faith, he needed a dacint washing. It's a long time since he had one. But come, boys, the bonfires are blazing, and we must put a carousin' cap on the May Day.

ROSALEEN. G'long wid ye! I'll follow ye whin I put Shevaun's shawl around me.

RODY. Begorra, Rosaleen, I'll stay till yer heart bids me go.

SHEVAUN. Wait for her.

(*Exeunt* DARBEY, SHEVAUN, *and* PEASANTS, C. D.)

RODY. How the divil could I lave ye, Rosaleen? The May-flowers are blooming to-day. Sure, darlint, they're jealous of yer purty cheeks and bright eyes, an' they're ashamed to show their heads, for you're the queen o' the May Day, and sure I love ye.

ROSALEEN (*music*). Sure, ye've tould me that same ould story over and over agin (*sad music*), but sure it makes me happy (*sadly*), so happy.

RODY. Ah, Rosaleen, you're sad agin. Like ould Erin, sure you're sad when you're cheerful, and ye smile wid the tears in yer eyes.

ROSALEEN. Ah, Rody, darlint, many the time when the tears were in me eyes, and the black throuble on me mind, have I smiled to make you happy.

RODY. Ye have. (*Kisses her.*) God bless ye, mavourneen! (ROSALEEN *sobs.*) There, don't cry, darlint! Sure, it will make your nose red. Tell me, acushla, what ye're thinking of. Sure, I'll lift the weight off your heart, just as I lifted Cassidy out of the window.

ROSALEEN. I was thinking, Rody, of what Cassidy said. I was wondering if he wuz telling the truth about Teddy Burke being murdered.

RODY. Niver fear, darlin', 'twas a great lie intirely. Sure, Cassidy never spoke a word o' truth in his live-long life.

ROSALEEN. He's thrying to pay ye back, Rody, for the poltogue ye gave him in the glen last night. Sure, it's the fear that's in me heart that you'll get in throuble for it yet.

RODY (*petting her*). There — there, asthore machree! It's the superstition that's coming over ye agin. Kiss me, and forget all about it. (*Kiss.*)

ROSALEEN. Oh, be off wid ye! Sure, ye're setting me poor heart upside down intirely. Ye'd better run off to the bonfire. I'll be after ye in a minute, when I get the shawl.

RODY. All right, mavourneen. (*Goes to door*, C. ; *aside*.) Sure, she's the purtiest posy that a gossoon could wear near his heart, my sweet Rosaleen.

(Exit C. *door.)*

ROSALEEN. It's gettin' dark. I'd better light the penny candle. (*Does so.*) May no harm come to my Rody. I'll pray to my mother at home (*looks up reverently*) to guard him from all danger. (*Going* R. 3 E.) I'll kneel down be Shevaun's bed an' pray that he'll be safe from all sorrow this blessed night.

(Exit R. 3 E. ; *stop music. Enter* SQUIRE ROSSMORE, C. *door.)*

SQUIRE. God save all — hello, deserted! (*Coming down* C.) I see all the villagers at the dance. I have just come from the cross-roads, and could not find Cassidy at the merry-making, the scoundrel! I did not dream that he would be capable of murder. Burke's body has just been found, washed up at the foot of Slieve Bwee, and Cassidy must have disappeared. I learned at the dance that he was seen to enter here a little while ago. No doubt the idiot is drunk. I must find him before his tongue has been loosened with alcohol. (*Starts up stage and encounters* ROSALEEN, *who enters* R. 3 E., *putting on shawl.*) Ah, Rosaleen, not at the dance, eh?

ROSALEEN. Miss O'Connor, sor, if ye plaze.

SQUIRE (*laughing*). Oh,·then, Miss O'Connor. I see you are proud of your name.

ROSALEEN. An O'Connor, sor, was the last King of Ireland. Squire Rossmore, ye are talking to another O'Connor.

SQUIRE (*aside*). Gad, she's spirited! (*Aloud.*) Quite true. Your pardon, Miss O'Connor. Realizing this fact, I have come to offer you an honorable alliance, worthy of your gentle self.

ROSALEEN. Sure, ye flatter me.

SQUIRE. 'Pon my honor, no; the statement of a fact is not flattery. Rosaleen, I —

ROSALEEN. Squire Rossmore, there is only one boy in the whole o' the county o' Cork that can call me Rosaleen in that loving way, and that boy is no less a person than your cousin Rody.

SQUIRE. A mere vagrant.

ROSALEEN. Stop, Squire! Rody thinks that it is better to be a rover, with the dogs and the children romping at his feet, and his heart full of love an' happiness, than to be a fine gintleman like yerself, with a pocketful of money and hated by all.

SQUIRE. Indeed! Very bad philosophy. Why, he's a mere beggar.

ROSALEEN. Rody the Rover is no beggar; he never begged a farthin' from ye in his life, and I know rather than do it he'd lay down on the flat of his back and die of starvation.

SQUIRE. Bombastic bosh!

ROSALEEN. Ah, ye may say so, but I know he'd rather be a beggar, and spend his last farthin' like a king, than be a king, and spend his last farthin' like a beggar.

SQUIRE. Come, come, Rosaleen, those words don't quite fit those pretty red lips of yours. (*Attempts to kiss her; enter* PA-TRICE, C. *door.*)

PATRICE. Cousin Maurice! (*He starts back.*) For shame!

SQUIRE. Patrice! A strange place for you.

PATRICE. No better place, surely, than under a roof where virtue dwells. (*Crosses to* ROSALEEN.)

SQUIRE. I must take my leave, to escape from those foolish and unpleasant platitudes. Good-morning, Miss O'Connor. A merry May Day to you. (*To* PATRICE.) I shall wait outside for you, cousin Patrice.

PATRICE. There is hardly a necessity. My brother Rody will escort me home. (*Exit* SQUIRE, D. C.) Tell me, Rosaleen, what he said to you.

ROSALEEN. He proposed to me very much after the style fine gintlemen propose to poor colleens who are below them in life.

PATRICE. You did not listen to him, did you?

ROSALEEN. Faix, Lady Patrice, what more could a poor colleen do? Me ears listened to him, but, sure, me heart all the time was only listening to the love of — of — (*Hesitates bashfully.*)

PATRICE. Of my brother Rody?

ROSALEEN. Yis; for sure I'll not hide it — it's no shame. I love him!

PATRICE. You're honest, Rosaleen. You are right — to love is no crime. Artificial society makes us ashamed of our love, but when you want to find human nature you must go among the poor and lowly.

ROSALEEN. True for ye, lady.

PATRICE. Rody'll be rich soon, Rosaleen.

ROSALEEN. Sure, I hope whin he is that he'll not be ashamed o' the poor colleen that gave him her heart's love when his coat was ragged and he did'nt have a ha' penny to buy a penny bun.

PATRICE. If he did that, he would be unworthy of you, Rosaleen. No matter how great one becomes, love makes us all the same. Love is a Democrat that levels all.

ROSALEEN. Democrat! Sure, I heard Misther Lawton, the American, say that every Irishman, whin he goes to Amerikay, becomes a Democrat.

PATRICE. There is an element of truth in that assertion.

ROSALEEN. Oh, then, all Irishmen fall in love whin they becomes Democrats.

PATRICE. With their party — yes; but really, Rosaleen, I'm at sea on American politics. I always thought that Democracy and Republicanism meant the same, but in America they think differently. Well, Rosaleen, both of you have a beautiful future before you, and not a cloud seems to mar the sunlit horizon of your lives.

(*Enter* SQUIRE, C. D.)

SQUIRE. I am waiting.

PATRICE. So am I, cousin, for my brother.

ROSALEEN. Step into the room, Lady Patrice, and I'll have Rody here in a minute. (*Goes* R. 3 E.)

PATRICE. I will. (*Exit* R. 3 E.)

ROSALEEN. If you'll be afther excusin' me, Squire, I must find Rody, as Lady Patrice wants to see him.

SQUIRE. Rody! Miss O'Connor, are you aware of the fact that Rody is under suspicion of murder?

ROSALEEN (*shrieks*). Oh — murder!

SQUIRE. Yes; Teddy Burke was found dead in the Shannon at the foot of Slieve Bwee over an hour ago. It seems that Rody was with him in Glen Blarney last night.

ROSALEEN. Yes, he was wid me; but what has that got to do wid murdher?

SQUIRE. It seems he was there alone afterwards.

ROSALEEN. Oh, surely, Squire, they don't think —

SQUIRE. That Rody committed the murder, eh? That is precisely what they do think.

ROSALEEN. Oh!

SQUIRE. Rody is under suspicion, and, if I am not mistaken, the police are now on their way here to arrest him.

ROSALEEN (*staggeringb ackwards, half dazed*). What! Arrest Rody — my Rody — for murdher! Oh, no no, no, Squire, it's a black lie! Sure, I was wid him in the glen last night, and we left there together.

SQUIRE. It is supposed that he murdered the American's servant, and robbed him of a box that contained a will which he thought would prove him to be the heir to my property.

ROSALEEN. Oh, sure, Squire, it's a lie! My Rody niver could do sich a thing!

SQUIRE. It seems that he declared to my man Cassidy last night in your presence that he meant to get possession of that will. Well, the holder of that will has been found dead He was murdered in the glen, and flung into the Shannon. Rody's stick, covered with blood, was found in the glen just now.

ROSALEEN. O Squire, I can't understand it at all! Me head is burnin' — I'll go mad! — mad!

SQUIRE. The circumstantial evidence is rather damaging, and I am afraid Rody will find it difficult to prove his innocence.

ROSALEEN. Oh, what is to be done? How can I help him?

O Squire Rossmore, sure, it's the powerful gintleman ye are.
Maybe it's yerself that could help him. Oh, pity me, do — do
(*kneels*), an' Heaven'll bless ye for it.

SQUIRE. Listen. I will make a bargain with you. I am rich
and powerful, as you say. I will send Rody to America.

ROSALEEN (*joyfully*). Oh!

SQUIRE. I have a steam-yacht at Barehaven. If he can reach
the coast, he may board that yacht and cross the channel to
France. From there he can take the French line steamer to
America.

ROSALEEN (*joyfully*). An' I will sail away wid him over the
blue wathers.

SQUIRE (*after going* R. 3 E., *returns*). No.

ROSALEEN. No?

SQUIRE. You must remain behind, and adorn my mansion with
your lovely presence.

ROSALEEN. O Squire —

SQUIRE. Rosaleen, can't you understand? Come to my home,
and jewels shall sparkle on that exquisite throat and bosom. Silks
shall rustle where those ragged garments now hang. Why, you'll
be the richest lady in the county — envied by all.

ROSALEEN (R., *sadly*). Stop! Stop! Envied by all! Sure,
I'd rather be loved than envied. Sure, what would the likes o'
me be doin' wid silks and jewels? No, no, Squire, I'd rather be
the poorest colleen in the county, wearin' tattered dresses, an'
have little wild-flowers instead of jewels, an' have a clean conscience, than be the fine misthress o' the Blarney House, wid
Squire Rossmore for me masther.

(*Music till end of act.*)

SQUIRE. Say, rather, your slave, Rosaleen. (*Starts to kiss
her.*)

ROSALEEN. Oh! (*Starts back* L.)

(*Enter* CORKERRY, C. D.; *he makes a straight walk down* C.,
then turns abruptly and marches R.)

CORKERRY (*loudly*). Hit's hall right, Capt'n. Hit's only the
Squire an' a bloomin' pretty lass.

(CUDDEEN CASSIDY *appears at window in flat.*)

SQUIRE (*surprised*). Cassidy! You here?

CUDDEEN (*aside to* SQUIRE). Whist! For the love o' Heaven
be aisy! (*Aloud.*) It's the police I have here, to arrest the murdherer o' Teddy Burke.

ROSALEEN (L.). Oh! (*Aside.*) I must run and tell Rody to
take to the hills.

(*Enter* PATRICE, R. 3 E.)

PATRICE (*surprised*). What's this?

ROSALEEN. O Lady Patrice, it's your brother that's in trouble this blessed night! Oh, I must tell him! (*She starts for* D. C., *and is stopped by entrance of* CAPTAIN CASTLETON *and two policemen.*)

CASTLETON. Not so fast, my girl. First tell us where we can find your friend — Rody, commonly called the Rover.

ROSALEEN. O Captain, agrah, ye don't mane to take him away from me? Ye're not going to put the irons on his hands? Oh, sure, it's breakin' me heart ye'll be, for I love him. Sure, he's my life, my love — an' soon we are to be married.

(CUDDEEN *crawls in and takes his place* R.)

CASTLETON. I am exceedingly sorry for you, my poor girl, but the iron hand of justice has crushed the life out of many hearts as gentle as yours. (*To* SQUIRE.) Ah, Squire, you are here to witness the arrest.

SQUIRE. No; merely a curious observer at the peasants' merrymaking.

CUDDEEN (*coming forward to* ROSALEEN). Ye'd better be afther telling, Miss Rosaleen darlin', where is Rody.

(*Enter* SHEVAUN, C.)

SHEVAUN. Arrah, what's this — the peelers in me house! Oh, murther! O Captain, agrah, ye may have all the whiskey in the house, if you'll only lave the roof over me head.

CORKERRY (*aside*). That's a bloomin' bargain I'd make with hall me 'art if I wuz Capt'n o' the Royal Hirish Constabulary.

CASTLETON. We're not looking for illicit whiskey, my good woman.

CUDDEEN. No; we're lookin' for Rody the Rover.

CORKERRY (*aside*). Hi don't like that Hirishman. He's got a face like a weazel suffering from congestion of the liver.

CUDDEEN. Shevaun, ye'd better be tellin' us where is Rody the Rover.

SHEVAUN. Oh, follow yer nose and find him.

CASTLETON. He must have escaped.

CUDDEEN. Yis; he tuck to the hills. He was too great a coward to face the music.

PATRICE. Gentlemen, my brother is no coward.

ROSALEEN. He is innocent of crime, an' has no raison to run away.

(RODY *appears at door; peasants crowd up behind him.*)

CUDDEEN. He has left the village.

RODY. It's a lie! (*All start; he comes in.*) Rody the Rover is here, an' is ready to meet any charge an' prove his innocence before the whole world. (*Folds his arms,* c. *stage; peasants crowd in doorway; two policemen keep them back by crossing their swords.*)

CASTLETON (*to* RODY). My young friend, rest assured I am very sorry to be the means of communicating to you the unpleasant fact that you are accused of the murder of Edward Burke.

RODY. What! Murdher! I'm accused of murdher! Who are me accusers?

CASTLETON (*pointing to* CASSIDY). There stands one. (*Showing stick.*) Here is the other.

RODY. My blackthorn!

CASTLETON. Then it is yours — you admit it!

RODY. Why, yis, Captain, that's mine.

CASTLETON. This stick was used to murder Edward Burke.

RODY. My stick? Why now I know. I left it in the glen last night.

CASTLETON. Ah, you also admit you were in the glen.

RODY (*surprised*). Why, yis.

CUDDEEN. See, Captain, he admits that he is the murderer.

CASTLETON. Silence!

CORKERRY (*flinging* CUDDEEN *aside*). Silence in the court! Keep your bloomin' face closed.

SQUIRE. The circumstantial evidence is quite strong, Captain.

CASTLETON. Quite strong. If we can prove a motive for the murder, it will be stronger.

RODY. Motive! Sure, what raison would I have for murdherin' a poor boy like Teddy Burke, an' have his gray-haired old mother to keen for him? Why should I kill him?

CASTLETON. To obtain possession of a will of which he was the possessor. He held it for Mr. Lawton.

RODY. Ye mane me uncle's will?

CUDDEEN. Yis; ye said last night that ye meant to get it, an' prove yerself the thrue owner of the Rossmore estate.

RODY. I did! Oh, I see it all now — I see it all! You, Cassidy — you are behind all this, an' maybe me fine Squire there! But I haven't the will.

SQUIRE. It's gone.

RODY. O Captain, agrah, I'm innocent!

CUDDEEN. As the jail-bird behind the bars.

RODY. Cassidy, if it takes till the Day of Judgment, you'll be paid back for this night's dirty work, believe my word!

CASTLETON. I am sorry for you, Rody. I sincerely hope you may clear yourself; but my sympathy must not interfere with my duty — you are a prisoner, arrested for murder. (SHEVAUN *begins to cry.*)

SHEVAUN. Oo! Oo!

RODY *and* ROSALEEN. Oh, no, no! (ROSALEEN *weeps.*)

CASTLETON (*to police*). Arrest him.

(*Two officers come forward and arrest* RODY.)

CASSIDY. Ah, ha, Rody! I said I'd pay ye back wid compound interest, but I niver dreamt ye'd bring the curse of the law on yer head for murdher.

RODY (*breaking away and striking* CUDDEEN). Murther! (CUDDEEN *falls* R.) Take that, an' I wish the shackles wor on my hands an' the rope on my neck for riddin the country of a snake like yourself.

(*Police seize him again,* C.)

ROSALEEN. O Rody, Rody!

RODY. Rosaleen, darlin', they're tearing ye away from me, *mo sthore, mo chree!* Don't mind, darlin', don't cry, Rosaleen ; sure, yer tears'll break my heart! (*Warn curtain.*)

ROSALEEN. O Rody, sure the light is lavin' me eyes! My heart is breaking — oh! (*Falls in swoon,* C. RODY *catches her in his arms.*)

RODY (*crying*). Rosaleen! Rosaleen! O Captain, it's mighty hard intirely. Sure, there's a lump in me heart. Look at that pale face there — look! Sure, the color is lavin her purty cheeks ; ye've broken her heart. Oh! (*He cries as they drag him away.* PATRICE *bends over* ROSALEEN.)

CURTAIN.

ACT III.

SCENE. — *A room in the Blarney House. Entrances,* C., R. 3 E., *and* L. 2 E. *Window entrance,* R. 1 E. *Sofa,* L. C. ; *table and chairs,* R. C., *front* ; *lamp lit on table ; decanter, glasses, etc.* SQUIRE ROSSMORE, *in smoking gown, discovered seated at table,* R. C., *drinking at curtain ; lights half down ; music tremolo.*

SQUIRE. I have lived a novel since the discovery of that murder. Cassidy made a colossal mistake in murdering that servant. I suppose he only meant to rob him, and to conceal his crime he had to commit a greater one. An innocent man has been arrested. and will suffer. He will be legally murdered. Thus one crime begets another. There is some strange and inexorable law in the universe on that point that human philosophy cannot fathom. Strange! (*Pours out brandy.*) Ha! I'm actually moralizing. (*Drinks.*) Events, however, have taken a good course. Circumstantial evidence is strong against Rody, and it will wind its legal red tape around the poor devil until it is drawn so tight that it will squeeze the life out of him. When he is removed (*rises*), then will there be no fears for the future. (*Crossing to* L..) Maurice Rossmore will be the only heir to this estate, and Rosaleen O'Connor will be a lonely girl badly needing the protecting wing of one who can raise her from the slough of poverty where the Irish people are rotting to this day. Why should I regret it? It is self-defence — the first law of nature. (*Crossing to window.*) Cassidy should be here by this time. He hid the box in the glen, and went to get it. He's got a heart of iron, and superstition seems to be dead in him. Why is he not here? How nervous I am! It's near day. (*Seats himself; knocker heard outside.*) Hello! The knocker! (*Rises.*) That is not Cassidy. He's got a key. (*Going* C.) Who the devil can be calling at this hour? (*At* C. D.) The steward is opening the door. (*Looks* L..)

LAWTON (*outside loudly*). I must see him! I insist! Stand aside or I'll carve the map of Ireland on your face!

(*Enter* LAWTON, C., *excitedly.*)

SQUIRE (*stepping back* R). Well, sir? Whom have I the honor to thank for this unwelcome visit?

LAWTON. My name, Squire Rossmore, is Lawton.

SQUIRE. The American?

LAWTON. Yes. I have just returned from Cork City. Necessity knows no law, social or otherwise. That is why I am here at this unconventional hour. I want to see you.

SQUIRE. To the point, if you please. What am I to understand?

LAWTON. Simply this. A cousin of yours, whose future destiny has been placed in my hands by his uncle, has been arrested on a false charge of murder. He was accused by your servant Cassidy. Well, that boy is innocent.

SQUIRE. Well, what has this got to do with me?

LAWTON. Everything. There was a deep and hidden motive in that accusation. The only man to be benefited by the possession of that will was yourself.

SQUIRE. Do you dare to think —

LAWTON. Think! I never think! It makes me perspire to think; and the fact of it is — I have never perspired.

SQUIRE. You mean to insinuate —

LAWTON (*coming down*). That you are a damned scoundrel!

SQUIRE. Sir!

LAWTON. Keep your temper. You may explode like a dynamite shell, and destroy yourself. Excitement is not good for people living in glass houses; it may break them.

SQUIRE. Sir, you —

LAWTON. Gently, sir. Your mentality is in an unsettled state. (*Crossing to table,* R.) Come over and I'll settle it for you.

SQUIRE. Sir, this insolence —

LAWTON. Insolence? A very unpleasant word. Not at all, my dear sir. That is simply a plain way of speaking we have out in California. Pray take a chair; I want to quietly discuss this matter with you. (*Seats himself* R. *of table.*) Sit down, sir.

SQUIRE. (C.). By Heaven, sir —

LAWTON. Pray, don't swear. Damn it! It jars my nerves. (*Sternly.*) Sit down! Squire Rossmore, as your kinsman Rody's representative, I welcome you and request of you to seat yourself in his house. Sit down, sir, or by Heaven I'll give you a dose of California medicine that will fix you quicker than that given by a doctor. (*Takes out pistol.*) You see I carry my little bottle of leaden pellets right here. (*Lays it near him on table;* SQUIRE *seats himself reluctantly.*) There, you have saved yourself the very unpleasant duty of eating a couple of my peculiar pills. Now, jesting aside. Let us shake hands. (*They shake hands.*) There, now we feel better acquainted. My card. (*Takes out card and hands it to* SQUIRE.) "Mr. Edward Lawton, Attorney-at-Law, San Francisco, California, U.S.A."

SQUIRE. My uncle died there.

LAWTON. Yes. One year ago, and appointed me his sole executor.

SQUIRE. Well?

LAWTON. He bequeathed this estate of which you are in possession to your Cousin Rody, known as "the Rover." My servant was murdered, and the box in which the will was has been stolen.

SQUIRE (*rising*). Then you have no means of disproving my claim to this property.

LAWTON (SQUIRE *seats himself again*). Now, have you any means of proving your claim to this property?

SQUIRE. Yes. A document left by my uncle before he left Ireland.

LAWTON. Have you it in your possession?

SQUIRE. Yes.

LAWTON. Of course you will show it to me.

SQUIRE. By what authority?

LAWTON (*touching pistol*). By the medical authority. Of course you respect such a profound authority. I would like to see that will.

SQUIRE (*rising*). It is in my bedroom. If you will wait here I will bring it to you.

LAWTON. Thanks; I will wait. (*Lights cigar and smokes.*)

SQUIRE (*taking lamp*). Excuse the lamp. (*Going to* C. D., *aside.*) I will also bring down a medical authority, and make him acknowledge the legality of my document, by setting the signature and approving the seal of my uncle's counsellor upon it.

LAWTON. I am waiting.

SQUIRE. You shall not wait long. (*Aside.*) Damn him! (*Exit* SQUIRE, C., *with lamp; lights three-fourths down.*)

LAWTON. The Squire is evidently praying for me. That game

of bluff went better than I expected. Irish gentlemen are evidently not used to the get-there-it-iveness of our countrymen. (*Looks out window.*) Hello! The moonlight has gone; it is getting very dark. Well, it is said that the darkest hour is always before the dawn. I hope so. (*Return to table,* R. C.)

(*Enter* L. 2 E. LADY PATRICE *with lamp; lights half up.*)

PATRICE. I thought I heard somebody talking here.
LAWTON (*surprised; rises*). Lady Patrice!
PATRICE (*startled*). Oh! Who's that?
LAWTON. Don't be afraid. It is I — Lawton, the American.
PATRICE (*relieved*). Oh! You startled me. (*Lays lamp on table.*)
LAWTON. No doubt my visit at this hour is unconventional, but the urgency of the case requires it. I am here to clear your brother from that terrible charge of which he is innocent.
PATRICE. That I know. Can you set him free?
LAWTON. Free! He is free. Free these three hours, though Squire Rossmore nor Mr. Cassidy does not know it as yet.
PATRICE. Thank God!
LAWTON. Of course when I read of the affair in the *Cork Examiner* last evening I hurried back and produced the will which it was alleged Rody had stolen. The charge was absurd. Rody had no reason to rob a man of something that was already legally his. I had it in my possession; and it belonged to Rody, and he knew it.
PATRICE. And he was released? Oh, how good you are!
LAWTON. It makes me happy to have you think so.
PATRICE. Oh, I see you already have the Blarney.
LAWTON. No; it was stolen. Lady Patrice, if that box contained the will, the only person that would have been benefited by it would be Squire Rossmore.
PATRICE. What! You surely don't think that —
LAWTON. Lawyers never think. Rody thinks that he has discovered the means to capture the real culprit. The last I saw of him was an hour ago. He went to Shevaun Jack's to borrow something. What it was I don't know.
PATRICE. I hope he will succeed.
LAWTON. I feel sure he will. (*Enter* C. CUDDEEN, *excitedly; he carries the little box and throws himself at* LAWTON'S *feet,* R. *Tremolo music.*)
LAWTON (*to* PATRICE *aside*). Leave the room! Quick!
PATRICE. Cassidy is mad! Heaven defend us! (*Exit* L. 2 E. LAWTON *lowers lamp on table.*)
CUDDEEN. Oh, for the love o' Heaven, Squire, save me — save me! He's afther me! Look, look! O Howly Mother, he's afther me!
LAWTON. Who?

CASSIDY. Teddy Burke! Teddy Burke! Look — look! He's pointin' his red fingers at me! He's lookin' at me wid those cold eyes! Oh! (*Shrinks.*) Sure, me soul is shrivellin' from their icy glance! O Squire, agrah, save me — save me! (*Grasps* LAWTON *around legs.*)

LAWTON. You've been drinking.

CUDDEEN. Yis — yis. Afther I left Shevaun's, I wint to the glin — to the glin where I murdhered him, to find the box and bring to ye.

LAWTON (*aside*). My God! The murderer! (*To* CUDDEEN) Go on! Go on!

CUDDEEN. Ah, I wuz afraid to pass the place, but I wint — I wint — there where I struck him down wid Rody's stick. I had barely tuk the box frum its hidin' place, whin who should lep out before me on the boheen, but Teddy himself in a white shroud.

LAWTON. Proceed!

CUDDEEN. Shure, I tuk to me two legs as if the divil wuz afther me — thim two eyes lookin' at me, and his white lips callin' me "murdherer! murdherer!" I turned wanst to strike him, but me hands struck nothin' but the air. 'Twas his ghost that was afther me. (*Enter* RODY, C., *disguised as* SHEVAUN *in a white nightdress and cap.*) Ha — there it is again! There it is again! (CUDDEEN *falls on floor weeping.*)

RODY (*imitating* SHEVAUN'S *voice and manner*). Sure, I followed Cuddeen Cassidy here. I thought I saw him robbing a reek o' turf in the glen, and I followed him. Egorra, I found the door open, and kem in.

LAWTON (*aside to* RODY). Hush! Hide inside that door there — quick! (*Points* R. 3 E.; *aloud.*) Shevaun, keep your ears sharp if you want to free Rody the Rover from murder.

RODY. Faix, I will that.

CUDDEEN (*resuming*). This crime is killin' me. It's atin' out me insides.

RODY (*aside to* LAWTON). Whist! He's talkin'!

CUDDEEN. I murdhered Teddy Burke because I was a desperate fool. Sure, I did it (God forgive me) to save me mother from starvation. (*Weeps on floor.*)

RODY. Glory be to goodness! Shure, he says he murdhered Teddy Burke.

LAWTON (*aside to* RODY). Hush! In there for your life, quick! (*Exit and re-enter* RODY, R. 3 E., *and talks from doorway.*) I'll write a brief note, telling the Squire I will return in the morning. (*Turns up light; scribbles a line on paper; lights up three quarters.*)

RODY. What'll Father Murphy think of a dacint, respectable widdy woman like meself in this dhress in the Squire's room at this hour o' the night? Oh, wirra! wirra! (*Exit* R. 3 E.)

LAWTON. Hark! The Squire is coming. I must go. (*Starts for* D. C.)

RODY (*poking head out door*, R. 3 E.). Ye're not going to lave me alone, are ye?

LAWTON (*at* C. D.). Silence! I'm off for the barracks to find the police. Hush! The Squire is coming! (*Exit* C. D.)

RODY. Oh, millhe murther, I'm disgraced intirely — I'm ruined — I've lost me kiractor. Father Murphy will raise the divil wid me next Sunday from the altar! Oh, wirra, wirra! ohone! What'll I do at all? Blood an' 'ounds, the Squire! Ohone! (*Exit* R. 3 E.)

(*Enter* SQUIRE, C.)

SQUIRE (*loudly*). There, my eccentric friend, is — (*Surprised.*) What, vanished — disappeared as quickly as he appeared. What's this? (*Reads note on table.*) "Will return in the morning. E. Lawton." I'm damned glad of it. Erratic character! He is the strangest — (*Sees* CUDDEEN.) Hello! Cassidy! The devil!

CUDDEEN (*half rising*). The divil! Yis, that's what I am! I'm in hell! Me tongue is parched, Squire; for the love o' Heaven give me a glass o' that brandy. I'm tremblin' like a lafe.

SQUIRE. You're drunk!

CUDDEEN. Yis; I've just come. (*Stretching out hand.*) The dhrink—the dhrink! (SQUIRE *pours out some brandy and gives it to him.*)

SQUIRE. There. You've been drinking too much already. You're as white as a ghost.

CUDDEEN (*drops glass*). Stop, stop, for the love o' Heaven! Teddy's ghost is hauntin' me.

RODY (*poking his head out of* R. 3 E.). Begorra, Cuddeen Cassidy is the first man that iver saw shnakes in Ireland.

CUDDEEN. Dhrops o' sweat are stramin' down all over me. Ah, but I got it — I got the box. I put a bottle o' courage in me first at Shevaun Jack's shebeen.

RODY (*pokes head out of door*). Whist! They're talking about meself.

SQUIRE (*seating himself* R. *of table*). Give me the box.

CUDDEEN. Give the pledge o' me mother's freedom from the poorhouse first— the money I mane.

SQUIRE. Cassidy, you've got the commercial instinct; you're a business man, I see. There are ten five-pound notes. (*Takes out money and hands it to* CUDDEEN.) Fifty pounds altogether.

CUDDEEN. I want a hundred! It's worth a big price.

SQUIRE (*taking out more money*). There are ten more; the bargain is closed.

CUDDEEN. There's the box, and the will. (*Lays box on table; takes money and folds it up.*) An' now, me fine buccho, we part company. (*Rises.*) I'm going to take me mother to Amerikay.

RODY (*aside*). God help us! She's dead!

SQUIRE (*to* CUDDEEN). Wait. Let us first examine the will. The box is locked.

CUDDEEN. Break it, as I broke Teddy Burke's skull. (*Takes out knife.*) There's me knife. (*Gives it to* SQUIRE.)

SQUIRE (*forcing box*). We shall see what the old fool's wishes were. (*Opens box;* CUDDEEN *and* SQUIRE *start back surprised; picture.*) What's this?

CUDDEEN. Murdher — where is the will?

RODY (*aside*). Ha, ha!

SQUIRE. There is no will. What's this? (*Takes out a little stone.*) A little stone!

CUDDEEN. A bit o' Blarney!

SQUIRE. A mere curiosity! Thunder and damnation! (*To* CASSIDY.) Idiot! Knave!

(*Enter* LADY PATRICE, L. 2 E.)

PATRICE. What is the matter, cousin?

SQUIRE. Leave the room, Patrice! Leave the room, I say, quick!

PATRICE. Oh! (*Exit* L. 2 E.)

SQUIRE. Cassidy, you meant to dupe me, to swindle me out of a hundred pounds for this stone. (*Drops it in box.*)

CUDDEEN (C.). I committed murdher to get that box. Ye've paid me to aise me conscience.

RODY (*aside*). Will the skies fall? Sure, they're having a business disagreement, an' the devil should be called in to decide it. (*Exit* R. 3 E.)

SQUIRE. Cassidy, you have not brought me that will; you have not earned the money. It belongs to me.

CUDDEEN (*pocketing it*). Possession is one of the nine pints o' law. Ye'll niver get it.

SQUIRE. I'll have you arrested for murder!

CUDDEEN. Ye can't; there'd be two of us.

SQUIRE (*seizing pistol from table*). Cassidy, hand over that money! Quick! (*Points pistol.*)

CUDDEEN. Ye coward!

(*Enter* ROSALEEN, C.)

ROSALEEN (*starting back*). Oh! (SQUIRE *and* CUDDEEN *look at her startled;* SQUIRE *drops pistol; picture.* SQUIRE R.; CUDDEEN L.; ROSALEEN C.)

ROSALEEN. I ax yer pardon for dhropping in so suddenly. I didn't know ye wor talking business. I jist left Teddy Burke's wake.

CUDDEEN. Teddy Burke's wake! Oh!

ROSALEEN. Yis. Iver since Rody's arrist I couldn't sleep, so I stepped over to the wake. There they tould me that Shevaun came over here, so I kem afther her.

SQUIRE. You did a rash thing. She is not here.

CUDDEEN. It's not here ye should be, me colleen. The wake is a more fittin' place for ye.

ROSALEEN. It's at the wake ye should be, more shame for ye. Ye have more cause to be there than any wan else.

CUDDEEN (*remorsefully*). What d'ye mane be that?

ROSALEEN. Why, don't ye know?

CUDDEEN. Know what? Spake out.

ROSALEEN. That yer poor mother died in the poorhouse to-night.

CUDDEEN (*dazed*). Me mother dead?

ROSALEEN. Yis.

CUDDEEN. No, no! It can't be; ye're lying.

ROSALEEN. It's the thruth I'm tellin' ye.

CUDDEEN (*seriously*). Then, Squire, all's over betune us. (*Takes out money and throws it at* SQUIRE'S *feet*, R.) There's yer dirty money, an' good riddins, for I'm goin' — (*Starts up stage*, C.)

SQUIRE. Going? Where?

CUDDEEN. To Father Murphy's to confession.

SQUIRE. And then?

CUDDEEN (*solemnly*). And thin — to join me mother in her grave!

SQUIRE. Cassidy, you're a fool!

CUDDEEN. Ah, I wuz a fool whin I murdhered Teddy Burke to plaze *you!*

ROSALEEN (*horrified*). Murdhered Teddy Burke! You! Oh!

SQUIRE (*desperately*). The ass is insane. His mother's death has turned his head.

CUDDEEN (*sadly.*) Thrue for ye, Squire Rossmore. It has turned me head (*looking upwards*) to where me mother's soul is now, I hope. Squire Rossmore, listen. I killed Teddy Burke to get that will for ye, so ye could destroy Rody's right to this property. Heaven has chated our designs, and taught me a greater lesson than wan of Father Murphy's sermons. (*Starts for* D. C.)

SQUIRE. You fool! Where are you going?

CUDDEEN. To the chapel first, to ax mercy from God; to the barracks afterwards, to ax no mercy from man! (*Exit* C.)

ROSALEEN (*horrified*). Oh! Rody's saved! God's will be done! (*Starts to exit*, C.)

SQUIRE. Stop, my pretty girl. You must not leave this room. (*Takes off smoking-robe and throws it across chair*, R.) If things are coming to this pretty pass, I must have one taste of happiness before I come to the end of my golden string. (*Starts to catch her.*)

ROSALEEN. Don't touch me! Help! help!

SQUIRE (*seizing her*). You're alone in my house at night!

(*Enter* RODY, R. 3 E.)

RODY. (C). It's a lie for ye! (*Throws off disguise, and flings* SQUIRE *aside.*) I'm here wid her.

SQUIRE. You! (*Starts back surprised*, R.)

ROSALEEN. Rody!

RODY (*clasping her*). Yis — the Rover! I'm the ghost that frightened the thruth out o' poor Cassidy. His neck'll make a purty fit for a collar made of a good stout rope.

SQUIRE. Scoundrel!

RODY. An' as for ye, me lovin' cousin, ye'll have to pay the piper that'll play at his wake.

SQUIRE (*seizing knife on table*). By Heaven! I'll pay you back before this game is up! (*Makes a rush at* RODY.)

ROSALEEN (*screaming*). Help! Oh!

(*Enter* CASTLETON, C., *followed by* LAWTON *and two policemen.*)

CASTLETON (*pointing pistol*). Drop it! Quick!

SQUIRE (*drops knife*). Damnation!

CASTLETON (*to policemen*). Arrest Squire Rossmore!

(*Two policemen advance and place* SQUIRE *under arrest*, R. C.)

RODY. Begorra, Columbus wuz right — the world goes around.

CASTLETON (*to* LAWTON, L.). Cassidy is already in custody. (*To* SQUIRE.) You are under arrest as an accomplice in the murder of Edward Burke.

SQUIRE. I?

CASTLETON. Yes; and also for fraud. You have no right to the possession of this property.

SQUIRE. The old Squire's will there proves my claim. None other exists!

LAWTON (*crossing* R. *to table*). Let me see that. (*Takes it up and looks at it.*) Like the man that owned it — false. It is a forgery. (*Tears it.*) Here is the real thing, left by old Rossmore. (*Takes out will.*) It proves Rody the Rover sole heir and owner of this property. (*Gives* RODY *the will.*)

CASTLETON. Remove the prisoner.

SQUIRE (*going out looking at* RODY). May ill luck attend you!

RODY. Squire, darlin', we'll keep your mimory green be watherin' it wid whiskey.

(*Exeunt* SQUIRE *and policemen* C. D. ; *enter* PATRICE, L. 2 E.)

PATRICE (*to* LAWTON). O Mr. Lawton, I'm glad you're here!

LAWTON (*going to her*). I've come to stay, at Rody's invitation.

CASTLETON (*to* RODY). I congratulate you, *Squire* Rody.

RODY. Thank ye, sor. (*Puts on* SQUIRE'S *robe.*)

CASTLETON. Good-morning. (*Exit* C.)

ROSALEEN. Rody, darlin', the dawn is appearing. Listen! The birds are singin' in the furze-bushes outside.

RODY (*taking her* R. C.). Shure, darlin', the sun'll rise as glorious as meself in a minute.

(*Enter* DARBEY DARNEY *and peasants,* C.)

DARBEY.   Sure, Rody, I wuz playin' at Teddy Burke's wake whin I heard the good news.   The top o' the mawernin', *Squire* Rody. Huroo for the County Cork and Blarney Castle!

PEASANTS.   Huroo! huroo!   (*Warn curtain ; lively dance music to accompany* DARBEY, *who begins to play the fiddle.*)

RODY.   What the divil are you doing, Darbey?

DARBEY.   Shure, I'm playing a new chune.

RODY (C., *taking up box from table, and taking out little stone*). Call it the " Bit o' Blarney."   Whoo!   (*All dance.*)

POSITIONS.

LAWTON *and* PATRICE, L. C.; RODY *and* ROSALEEN, C.; DARBEY *and fiddle*, R. C. ; *peasants at rear; picture; dance.*)

CURTAIN.

SCENE PLOT.

ACT I.

Full Stage: a Glen at night.

Night landscape drop, with winding river and castle.

River.	Castle. ☉	☉ Bunch
Low Rocks.		Light.
Rock wing.	Rocky run.	Tree.
Tree wing.	Furze Tree. ☉	Tree wing.
	Green Bank.	
	Green baize down; grass mats and flowers.	

NOTE. — Fix yellow flowers on tree R.C. every night.

ACT II.

Full Stage: a plain Kitchen (boxed).

Landscape Backing.

R. 3 E.

Low casement window to open.

C. Door.

Counter with liquors.

Cupboard.

Old-fashioned Fireplace.

Red ☉ Light.

Table and Chairs.

Table and Chairs.

L. 2 E.

Board floor; sand for dancing.

NOTE. — Have kettle covered with lampblack hanging in fireplace.

ACT III.

SCENE I. — Interior Office Flats in one.
SCENE II. — Full Stage: Fashionable Interior (boxed).

SCENE II.

Hallway Backing.

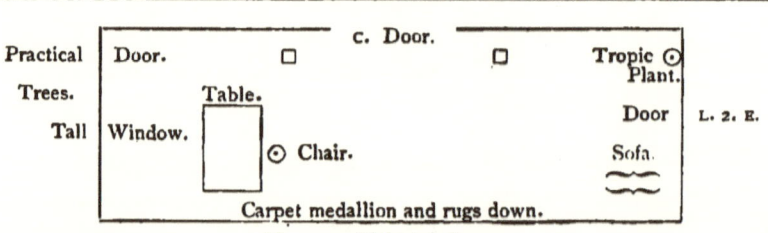

Practical Trees.

Tall

Door.

C. Door.

□   □

Table.

Window.   ☉ Chair.

Tropic ☉ Plant.

Door   L. 2. E.

Sofa.

Carpet medallion and rugs down.

NOTE. — Light two lamps.

A NEW ENTERTAINMENT FOR LADIES.

JOLLY JOE'S
LADY MINSTRELS.

Selections for the "Sisters."

Written, compiled and edited in the sole interest of cheerfulness, from the most jovial sources, and arranged with a particular eye to the needs of

FEMALE NEGRO MINSTRELS.

By Mrs. A. M. SILSBEE and Mrs. M. B. HORNE.

This little book describes the programme recently employed in an actual performance of this character, and is offered as a guide to others seeking light on this "dark subject." It provides jokes, a stump-speech, a darky play—"Bells in the Kitchen,"—written for female characters only, and suggests a programme of songs. The difficulty which ladies have found in collecting humorous material sufficiently refined for their purpose, and the impossibility of procuring an after-piece for this sort of entertainment, of which men have heretofore had a monopoly, suggested the publication of this book, which meets both these wants.

Price . . . . . 25 Cents.

A NEW DRAMA.

HICK'RY FARM.

A COMEDY-DRAMA OF NEW ENGLAND LIFE IN TWO ACTS.

By EDWIN M. STERN.

Six male, two female characters. A charming delineation of New England rural life, presenting a diversity of excellent characters, that of the farmer, Ezekiel Fortune, being particularly good. Scenery: a landscape, with small set cottage, and a plain room. Costumes of the present time. Time of playing, an hour and a half.

Price . . . . . 25 Cents.

PLANTATION BITTERS.

A COLORED FANTASY IN TWO ACTS.

By MARY B. HORNE,

AUTHOR OF

" PROF. BAXTER'S GREAT INVENTION," " THE GREAT MORAL
DIME SHOW," ETC.

Nine male and eight female characters, all impersonated by men and boys.
Scene, an easy interior ; costumes, grotesque and easily contrived. This is a
picture of negro life on the Abercrombie Plantation, in Georgia. It is a very
humorous presentation of negro life and character, and provides an agreeable
substitute for the hackneyed Negro Minstrel Entertainment. It is connected by
a thread of narrative, but chiefly consists of a succession of songs and humorous
incidents, affording ample opportunities for the introduction of specialties. An
excellent entertainment for a lodge-room or other "stag" institution. Can be
played by men and women, if preferred. Very funny and perfectly inoffensive
for church performance.

Price . . . . . 15 cents.

ST. VALENTINE'S DAY.

A COMEDY IN ONE ACT.

By ANNIE ELIOT.

Two female characters. Scenery, unimportant ; costumes modern and every-
day. This charming little duologue for ladies will instantly recommend itself to
the best taste in such matters. Its dialogue is witty, ingenious and entertaining
and very subtly and sympathetically develops a most interesting story of a love
affair, which, however, only appears in the third person. The characters of
Elinor (a woman of thirty) and Letty (scarcely more than a child) are admirably
contrasted and employed, and are capable of much quiet dramatic effect in
capable hands.

Price . . . . . 15 cents.

A NEW PLAY FOR GIRLS.

THE CHAPERON,

A COMEDY IN THREE ACTS,

By RACHEL E. BAKER,

PART AUTHOR OF "AFTER TAPS," ETC.

Fifteen female characters. Scenery not difficult. Costumes, tennis gowns
and modern street and evening gowns, with picturesque
Gypsy costumes for Miriam and Jill. Time
in playing, two and a half hours.

Price . . . . . . 25 cents.

SYNOPSIS:

ACT 1. JACK AND JILL. A love game. Cousins for sale. "My kingdom for
a hairpin." The French teacher. A few conundrums. Miriam and Jill.
The Gypsy's blessing. Nora and the French language. *Billet-doux* and
Billy Manahan. An invitation. "I will be your chaperon!" Telling for-
tunes. THE TENNIS DRILL. Tales out of school. Joyce and the beggars.
The accusation. Joyce to the rescue. "I cannot look into your eyes and
believe you guilty." Under a cloud. The Gypsy's prophecy. "Miriam the
Gypsy has spoken, and she never breaks her word."

ACT II. THE CHAPERON. In the studio. Nora and the man in armor. A
spiritual manifestation. Eavesdropping, Locked in. The artist's model.
A little lark. The bogus chaperon. The skeleton in the closet. Romeo
and Juliet adapted. Miriam the Gypsy. The secret of the papers. "God
be with them and with those to whom they belong!" Masquerading.
Nora's jig. A surprise and an escape. The school-ma'am outwitted. THE
MINUET. Jill and Joyce. The locket. "It means that the waif has found
a home at last!" Sisters. The Gypsy again. "Your duty lies with them
make their lives as happy as you have mine."

ACT III. "LIKE OTHER GIRLS." A five o'clock tea. Anticipations. The
French teacher again. A lesson in politeness. A nice hot cup of tea.
Nora's revenge. Apologies. Mademoiselle's confession. "I took it; it was
only for ze revenge." Forgiveness. "*Rushing* tea." Confessions. From
grave to gay. An Adamless Eden. Superfluous man: a few portraits of
him. Explanations. The fulfilment of Miriam's prophecy. A mystery
cleared. "The little one I mourned as dead is alive." Our chaperon,

COUNSEL FOR THE PLAINTIFF.

A COMEDY IN TWO ACTS.

By ST. CLAIR HURD.

For four male and five female characters. Scenery, two interiors, easily arranged; costumes modern and simple. ' Plays an hour and a half. This little piece has more plot than is usual in plays of its length, and works up to an exciting climax. Solomon Nathan is a capital comedy part, and Phineas Phunnel and Phœbe Stopper excellent eccentric character parts. This piece has been many times successfully performed from manuscript.

Price . . . . 15 cents.

FOR FEMALE CHARACTERS ONLY.

A VISION OF FAIR WOMEN.

A DRAMATIC PARAPHRASE IN ONE SCENE,

Based upon Tennyson's "Dream of Fair Women."

By EDITH LYNWOOD WINN.

(As presented by the Polymnia Society, of Shorter College, Rome, Ga., April, 1889.)

Thirty-nine girls are called for by the full text of this excellent entertainment, besides the "Dreamer" who has the vision; but a smaller number may be used, at pleasure, by simply reducing the number of tableaux. No scenery is required, and the costumes can be easily contrived by home talent. This is a very picturesque and enjoyable entertainment, and by giving a large number of pretty girls a chance to look their best, is sure to please them and every one else.

Price . . . . 15 cents.

WHO'S TO INHERIT?

A COMEDY IN ONE ACT.

FOR FEMALE CHARACTERS ONLY.

For nine female characters. Scene, an easy interior; costumes, modern and simple. Margery is a "rough diamond," who always speaks her mind. Miss Chatter, Miss Pry and Miss Nicely are a very amusing trio of gossips, to whom Mrs. Fitzfudge's sharp tongue is a terror.

Price , . . . 15 cents,

ANOTHER "COUNTRY SCHOOL."

THE OLD-FASHIONED

HUSKING BEE.

AN OLD FOLKS ENTERTAINMENT IN ONE SCENE.

By NETTIE H. PELHAM.

For eleven male and five female characters, and as many more as desired. Scene, the interior of a barn, easily arranged; costumes, old fashioned. Plays forty minutes or more, according to number of songs and specialties introduced. Very easy to get up, and very funny. An excellent introduction for a dance, supper or sociable, where a mixed entertainment is desired.

Price, ... 15 Cents.

SYNOPSIS:

SCENE. — Uncle Nathan's barn. Bobby and Scipio. In black and white. A few conundrums. "Silence am gold." Gathering of the neighbors. Music and fun. Thomas Jefferson is heard from. "Von leedle song," by Solomon Levi. Betsy and Josiah. A leap-year courtship. Algernon Fitznoodle and Little Lord Fauntleroy. The dude and the darling. Fitznoodle takes a tumble. Patrick and Ah Sin. Race prejudices. Harmony out of discord. Music. Betsy and the swing. A little mistake. Betsy recites. THE HUMANIPHONE. Pat and Kitty. The red ear. "Hurrah for supper!"

A DOUBLE SHUFFLE.

A COMEDY IN ONE ACT.

By HARRY O. HANLON.

Three male and two female characters. Scenery and costumes very simple. An admirable little parlor piece, playing about thirty-five minutes. Fred Somers, a collegian, with a taste for practical joking, tries to play a little joke on his sister and his fiancée, but they succeed in turning the tables completely upon him and his two college chums. Very bright and amusing. A sure hit.

Price, ... 15 Cents.

www.ingramcontent.com/pod-product-compliance
Lightning Source LLC
Chambersburg PA
CBHW022200020726
47496CB00008B/2813